The Submissive Scullery Maid

A Victorian tale depicting the life of Irish lass, Sally McGuire.

Shiralyn J. Lee

The Submissive Scullery Maid

Contact information:

Face Book-Shiralyn J Lee

Twitter-@ShiralynLee

ISBN-13: 978-1481983563
ISBN-10: 1481983563

The Submissive Scullery Maid

Contents

The Submissive Scullery Maid

Introduction

This is a Victorian story about Sally McGuire, an Irish girl who is forced to grow up in an orphanage after the untimely death of her mother. As soon as she is able to, along with her friends, she leaves her homeland behind her in hopes for a better future in England.

Sally quickly settles in to her new job, working for Mr. Forbes and his sister. Enduring snide remarks from Mr. Brookes, who is head of staff, she is determined to prove to him that she is a worthy employee. But her position in the house is cut short as Mr. Forbes and his sister are to move back to America, their homeland. Sally soon finds employment as a scullery maid working for Mr. and Mrs. Cox, a very wealthy and well to do couple in their social circles. They have employed Sally to work in their London City house and Mrs. Cox has taken an instant liking to the red headed girl. But dark secrets and lies tie Sally to Mrs. Cox in a way that no one would ever suspect. Sally is quickly drawn into a world of fetish fantasies, with her employer at the helm. Mrs. Cox, or Lidia as she is known to Sally during their secret meetings, manages to seduce her employee and take her mind, body and soul to places that she never knew existed. This story will captivate you and tantalise your mind as you become acquainted with Sally and her mistress during the time where the White Chapel Murderer, or more commonly known as Jack the Ripper, claimed his victims.

Chapter One

Sally was asleep in her makeshift bed, something that she and her mother had attempted to put together. It was just a few dirty old woolen blankets covering a small pile of yellow straw that acted as a mattress, where she occupied a tiny space in the corner of the single room that they could barely afford to rent. And that was all that she and her mother had to live in, a small room that was dark and gloomy, built with grey stones that formed the four walls and pieces of broken slate that covered the ground.

Every now and again Sally would find herself face to face with a black rat that had come searching in hopes for any crumbs of food that she hadn't managed to properly sweep up. She would have to chase it outside with the broom, beating the ground as hard as she could to scare it away for good. It was a task that she hated but there was no one else to take charge when her mother had been taken seriously ill.

Sally had now reached her twelfth year in life and was mature beyond her age. She had been the adult in this home for some time now, as her mother had slowly fallen ill from a venereal disease that she had contracted through prostitution. It was the only way that she had been able to provide food and shelter for her and Sally and now that she was bedridden, it would just be a matter of time before Sally herself would have to succumb to such terrible acts in order to survive and keep herself from being sent to the workhouse.

It was a dark, cold morning, the rain had turned to icy sleet and Sally shivered beneath her blanket as she blew her breath over her fingers to try and keep them warm. She heard her mother cough and peeked out to see if she was ailing any worse than she did yesterday. Deep down,

1

she knew that there wasn't much time left with her mother and she would have to find a way to make a shilling or two if she wanted to stay alive herself.

"Sally, Sally," her mother croaked from her bed.

"I'm coming, ma. Just you hush now and save ya strength."

Sally wrapped the blanket around her tiny shoulders—pinching it tightly together just below her chin. Her long red hair tousled down her back with pieces of straw sticking out here and there but she had no time for grooming, she knew that her mother's calling was not that of someone who would take advantage of the situation. No, if her mother called her, it meant that she was in great pain and in need of help.

"Sally, it's time. I'm ready to go now," she told her daughter. She was lain on her back and winced in agony as she released a second cough.

"Ma, just you be quiet, now. There's plenty of time for such talk. When you get better we can go for walks along the shore-line and watch the seagulls fly above and fight over any scraps of food they might find."

Sally had tears in her eyes and she found it hard to choke back her emotional state as she watched her protector grow even sicker. Holding her mother's cold boney hand, she patted it gently and began to tell her stories of how she was going to see the ocean with the waves cresting over and hitting the sand. And that one day soon, Prince Charming would come knocking on their door, confessing his undying love and whisking her away to a land where dreams really can come true. Sally was a big dreamer and believed from a very young age that she and her mother would be rescued from this dirty depressing city and taken to a place where they could live as royalty, or close to it. It was the only thing that kept her sane.

The Submissive Scullery Maid
Shiralyn J. Lee

As Sally went on to tell her story, she hadn't noticed that her mother's eyes were now closed and that she had taken her last moment of breath. But as soon as she felt her frail hand go limp, she knew that her mother had passed away and was reluctant to release her from her hold.

Tears fell from her eyes and rolled down her dirt ridden cheeks, leaving clean streaks where they had left their mark. She sniffed loudly and wiped the drips from her button red nose with the back of her hand. Although she was saddened that her mother had been taken, she was also grateful that she was now at peace with her maker. Sally had found it hard taking care of her mother and it had taken a toll on her health on more than one occasion. But now she would have to fight to survive and find work wherever she could. She concluded that she would have to pass herself off as older than she really was and get work at the first opportunity.

It was a week later and Sally still hadn't managed to find employment. She was tired, cold and practically starving, just barely surviving from any crumb of food that she could beg, borrow or steal. And now she had found herself on the same food chain level as the rats that she so hated.

It was still dark outside and she'd only been awake for a few minutes when there was a fierce loud knock on the door, causing Sally to tremble with fright.

"Open up in there. We know you're in there, Sally McGuire, now let us in!" a man's husky voice bellowed from behind the wooden door.

Sally, standing at the door with her ear pressed hard against it, listened intently for any kind of movement. "Who are ya, what d'ya want?" she cried out to him.

The man banged again. "We've come to take ya to the orphanage an' ya had better come along quietly, lass."

The Submissive Scullery Maid
Shiralyn J. Lee

Sally was shaking with fear. She couldn't go to the orphanage, not now. She had to find work.

"Why are ya takin' me to the orphanage, I'm too old to go, you've have made a mistake?" she called out as she pressed the side of her face even harder against the door, trying to listen to what he was saying to her neighbour. She could only hear mumbled voices but she knew that her neighbour hated children, especially girls, so whatever he was saying, wasn't going to benefit her.

There was another heavy pounding noise on the door and then it suddenly flung open, causing Sally to fall back on to the slate floor. Two men came barging in. One was a tall and skinny man with a long boney jaw line and deep set eyes with black circles beneath them and the other man was short and fat and stank of whisky.

"Now, now, Sally, you are a little ting, aren't ya. There won't be much of a to-do with you, will there, now miss," the fat man said smugly as he rubbed his bristly fat cherub cheek.

Sally tried to run around the table and make her escape but before she was able to reach the doorway the tall man stretched his arm out in front of her, grabbing her by her hair. He tugged on it hard and yanked her back so forcefully that she fell to the ground at his feet, kicking and screaming.

"Leave me alone, get offa me, help me, somebody help me," she screamed, hoping that one of her neighbours would come running in and give these mongrels a good hiding. But her prayers went unanswered and she was held against her will.

As she struggled to break free from the firm grip, she was frog marched out into the hallway and down the narrow staircase where she bashed her face twice into the wall through no lack of trying to run for it

The Submissive Scullery Maid
Shiralyn J. Lee

"Get in there and keep ya trap shut," the tall man sniggered as he opened the back of a small black carriage and lifted her up into it, closing the door and locking it behind her.

Sally held on to the iron bars in a small opening that prevented her from escaping. As the carriage moved away, she could see her neighbours standing on the side pavement, looking guilty for allowing her to be taken away in such a horrid manner.

She could hear the two men talking as they sat up front acting like they'd just captured the prize pig. Their voices were muffled but she thought that she distinctly heard them talking about how much they had achieved by removing the filthy poor from the streets and throwing them in to the workhouse where they could be put to good use.

One of them laughed out loud and then banged on the front of the carriage and called out, "Hey, little miss, we got a right good penny for getting you."

Sally sat back on the narrow wooden bench that had been fitted to the side. She noticed a stench, it smelt like urine and it made her want to throw up. Her fate was now in the hands of the cruelest people that she could imagine.

The horses had maintained a trot pace and it had taken about twenty minutes to reach the orphanage. But to Sally, it looked more like a prison house. There was a large wrought iron gate with chain links that were attached to the six foot stone wall and then wrapped around the spindles and a large padlock to keep the children within its boundaries. The red-brick orphanage was huge, plain and boring in its appearance and filled with many children.

The carriage came to a halt and Sally could hear footsteps approaching the back door. She heard keys rattling followed by one of them being turned in the lock. The small door swung open and the two

5

men—grinning and rubbing their hands together, told her to hurry up and get out.

"Hope you'll be very comfy in your new home," the fat one giggled.

"Now ya can join all the other unwanted bastards. No one wants you, you're all like vermin, the lot of ya. It would do this great community a good service if you'd all died at birth," the tall man said with superiority in his voice.

Sally was in no position to argue, so dejectedly, she kept her head down and continued to walk slowly in the direction of the building. The two men escorted her on either side and keenly helped her on her way by holding on to each of her elbows, informing her that she was at St. Bridgette's Orphanage for children, where she was going to be spending the next few years.

"Bring the wretched chiseler in and take her to the office. Sister Lynch will want to speak to her right away," a large woman in a nun's habit ordered.

She was taken inside and then marched straight down a narrow corridor until they arrived outside of Sister Lynch's office. The fat man wiped his hands on his dirty green jacket and then knocked hard on the door with his knuckles. A female voice—stern and callous sounding, told them to enter.

"Ah, Mr. O'Doherty and Mr. Quinn, I see that you have bought me yet another bastard child off the streets." She sighed heavily to show that the very nerve of the girl's presence had inconvenienced her. "Very well. I suppose I can make room for yet another. You may leave us now, gentlemen, I have no further use for your services." Then directing her attention toward Sally, her eyes changing to a piercing stare, she picked up a pencil and began to tap it on the edge of the desk. "Child, take your place in front of my desk and make sure to be silent." She opened up a large brown ledger and licking her finger, she turned several pages until she reached the one she was looking for.

6

The Submissive Scullery Maid
Shiralyn J. Lee

She wrote down the date and Mr. O'Doherty and Mr. Quinn's names. "Still here, gentlemen?" she asked with her attention still buried in the ledger.

The two men tipped their hats and stepping backwards, walked out of the office, leaving a very fragile girl alone and petrified. Sally maintained her silence. It would not benefit her to speak at this point in time.

"So when I ask you a question, you will answer it immediately, do you understand?" Sister Lynch looked up from her desk at the pathetic bag of bones and tutted at the girls' appearance.

Sally clasped her hands together in front of her and nodded her head.

"Do you have a tongue, child, or did someone already answer my prayers and cut it out. I asked you a question, head gestures are not permitted unless advised by me and you will call me Sister Lynch. Now what is your name?"

"Sally McGuire, Sister Lynch," she mumbled.

"When were you born, not that I expect you to know when your floosie mother gave birth to you?"

"December 12th 1870, Sister Lynch," Sally answered quickly.

"Where did you live?"

Sally looked down at her feet. "Kildare Street, Dublin, Sister Lynch."

Sister Lynch picked up a bell that had been placed to one side of her desk. She rang it loudly. The sound of heels tapping, could be heard as someone came running down the corridor, heading straight for the office. A young nun quickly entered the room. She looked solemn as she waited for her instructions.

Sister Lynch closed the ledger. "Take this child to ward three."

The Submissive Scullery Maid
Shiralyn J. Lee

"Yes, Sister Lynch," the nun replied—her voice fragile and her body language showing how nervous she was.

She took Sally by her arm and kept her silence whilst they walked along the corridor and up two flights of concrete stairs.

"Now that we're out of Sister Lynch's earshot we can talk. I'm Sister Catherine and I usually run around doing errands for Sister Lynch. The old battle-axe has me dartin' all over the place some days. You had better be warned now though, if you upset her enough, the entire building will shake from fear of her screams. Some of the children make up secret songs about her and sing Sister Lynch will be lynched."

"Thank you for your kindness, Sister Catherine, you are the first person to show me any crumb of sympathy today," Sally humbly said to her.

"Believe me, child, there's not a lot of that around here, so you better get used to it."

They hurried to the ward where Sally was to call this her home for the next three years and Sister Catherine showed her directly to her bed.

There was no heat in the ward and each bed consisted of only one grey woollen blanket. There were fifty beds in total, all stacked next to each other with just a few inches between each one for access. Sally felt sad, frightened and lonely but under no circumstances was she going to allow herself to show the others how fragile that she was actually feeling. Her mother had shown courage right up until her last breath and that was what Sally was going to do.

"The priest will be visiting us tomorra, so best behaviors all around. Now Sister Lynch will expect you to work whilst you're here, so first ting in the mornin' be down stairs and make sure you're clean and tidy. It's going to be harsh for you, Sally, at least for a while anyway, so be sure to make friends as soon as you can now."

Sister Catherine left her sitting on the edge of her bed. Sally sat with her feet just barely touching the floor and not daring to move. The door opened and she was soon surrounded by a group of girls her own age.

"Oh, we have a new guest at the Inn. You'll be staying in this establishment a while then, won't you," one of them said, poking fun at her.

"Never mind that gobshite. She wets the bed, don't ya, Addie Brannon. I'm Eveleen and this is Mary and Margaret."

"Hello, I'm Sally, Sally McGuire," she said quietly, feeling slightly at a slight disadvantage.

"Nice to meet ya, Sally McGuire." Eveleen said smiling sweetly. Although she was an extremely skinny girl she had an air of attractiveness about her. Her long black curly locks flowed over her shoulders and down her back, ending at her waistline, and her eyes were piercing blue circles, made extra prominent by her white porcelain skin.

Sally felt a warm sensation inside her belly when she conversed with Eveleen. She didn't understand why but assumed that it could possibly be that she was drawn to her kind voice, as she had heard so little of this type of behavior recently.

"We best be goin'. We don't want Sister Lynch to beat us if we don't finish our chores. That daft biddy would have us working day and night if we didn't need ta sleep. Maybe you should come with us and get used to the grueling work load. No one is safe from the wrath of her work load," Mary informed her.

They took her downstairs and showed her what she would be expected to do. Laundry was first on the list. This would take hours to complete. There were hundreds of bed sheets to wash and hang out to dry and many girls were working hard to make sure that they were all washed and dried before dusk. Once this was done, they folded the sheets and then cleaned up ready for supper.

The food hall was huge and tables were lined up in rows from one end to the other. At least one hundred children could sit and eat at one given time. Sally was seated next to Eveleen and not one child spoke a word during their meal. After finishing up they formed an orderly line and carried their plates to a table at the end of the room, where they would be collected and taken to the scullery to be washed by several girls who had been placed on duty.

"Make sure you get plenty of sleep, Sally. Today was easy for ya but tomorra will be a different story. They'll have us all working seven days a week from dawn to dusk and very little time to even think," Eveleen whispered to her.

They were all ordered to their wards and soon afterwards every child was laid in their bed and covered in their single blanket. Sally compared this bed to the one that she'd been sleeping in at home. So far this one was better. She quickly fell asleep and with Eveleen in the bed next to her she found that she felt a little safer tonight.

The following morning Eveleen woke Sally up at 6am. It was still dark outside but neither girl had time to hang about. Along with most of the other girls, they quickly dressed and made their way downstairs to start their working day. Sally was unsure of her role, as so many orders were being thrown at her at one time.

"Wash these sheets."

"Clean the windows."

"Set the tables."

She moved as quickly as she possibly could but she still managed to catch the attention of one of the nuns who happened to be on duty standing by the back wall. She had a scowling face and gave the impression that she would rather beat you than have to speak to you.

"Sally McGuire, just because you're a new girl here, doesn't mean to say that you can get away with very little work chores. Do you hear me?" Sister Agnes yelled at her.

Sally was practically running from one chore to another but she could still feel Sister Agnes's eyes burning into her as she watched her like a hawk. Just as she was picking up her pace, as well as trying to maintain precision, one of the other girls dropped a pile of plates that she had just picked up and attempted to carry across the scullery. The entire room fell silent. The poor girl was surely going to be punished for this mess. Sally went to bend down to help pick up the pieces but Eveleen held her arm, stopping her immediately. She gave her a look as though she was telling her not to move without permission. The nun walked right up to the girls' face and glared at her as if she wanted to murder her. Sally could see that this girl was petrified to the point of wanting to die on the spot.

"You are going to pay for your sins, Finola O'Conner. Fetch me that chair right now." She pointed in the direction of a wooden seat and tapped her foot whilst she waited impatiently. Finola carried the chair and stood in front of Sister Agnes, waiting for orders of where to put it. "Place it behind me and then wait."

Finola put the seat on the ground behind the Sister and began to shake uncontrollably. She had seen how cruel Sister Agnes could be when she had been angered and at any moment now, she would endure a savage punishment. Sister Agnes sat in the seat and then pulled a wooden hairbrush from her pocket and held it out like a trophy. She pointed to her lap and Finola draped herself over the black skirt, ready to take her beating. Sister Agnes raised her arm into the air and then began the wicked thrashing. Finola screamed out, as each whipping stung more than the last one and the more that she wriggled and screamed, the harsher the beating became. All that the other girls could do was stand and watch and keep silent. Sally held her fists in a tight grip at her sides. She was angered at the display that seemed to be a normal daily act for this nun. She wanted to give Sister Agnes a damn good thrashing and show her how it would feel to be humiliated for an act that held no malicious content.

After a few minutes, Sister Agnes was still beating the girl and by the looks of it she seemed to be revelling in it and the only reason that she stopped was because Sister Catherine had been informed of the pasting and came running to Finola's aid. She managed to coax Sister Agnes to stop her act of violence and lifted the injured girl from her assailant. Finola was taken away and her sobbing could be heard for quite some time after she disappeared out of sight. Sister Agnes ordered Sally to put the chair back in its original place and then stood back in the same spot as before and carried on watching the girls fulfilling their chores. Her face was red and perspiring and her breathing heavy and deep but she still managed to maintain that evil wicked expression.

"Just remember that suffering is good for you and you should give it up as penance for your sins," she scorned at them. Sadly this was a repetitive chant that several of the nuns would quote when they felt that the girls could possibly find reason to challenge their motives.

The girls immediately set to their tasks, each one afraid to drop or break anything.

"This happens on a daily basis, Sally. We're all destined for the beatings from that evil cow," Eveleen whispered into her ear.

"She'll get what's due to her all in good time," Margaret quietly butted in. "God help anyone who wets their bed. She has them parade around wrapped in their wet sheets so we can all gawk at them. She has a cruel heart, they all do and I hope they are the ones who pay for their wicked sins one day."

After the laundry had been put away and the dishes stacked in their piles, it was time to receive the priest on his monthly visit. All of the girls were gathered in the assembly hall and stood whilst he preached a sermon and informed them of their wicked sins.

"It's okay, one day you'll become immune to all of this. Just follow everyone else and take your mind to a place where you know that you can be happy. It's your only escape. Jaysus, there's not one fekkin girl in here who gives a damn about what he's gotta say," Eveleen said quietly to Sally.

Sally smiled and secretly placed her hand over Eveleen's. She had just realised that this girl was going to be an invaluable best friend to her.

The Submissive Scullery Maid
Shiralyn J. Lee

The Submissive Scullery Maid
Shiralyn J. Lee

Chapter Two

Time had not passed quickly enough for Sally and the past three and a half years had been filled with only soulless treatment from the nuns and hard labour for her and the other girls. If it had not been for the likes of Eveleen and her close friendship with her, Sally would surely have been driven crazy and sent to the mad house by now.

It was now December 1886 and Sally was readying to leave this stench that she was forced to call home. Eveleen had left a few weeks prior and promised that she would come and collect Sally on her final day.

Sally's heart was filled with excitement as she had only hours to go before she could depart from her tormentors. Margaret and Mary would soon be following her on their departure over the next couple of months but Sally held no hope for their future and pictured them soon to be prostitutes, destitute and at the mercy of any man who would pay them for their services. Sally was determined not to be forced into that position.

As like all the other girls, she had no possessions to take with her, just the clothes on her back but that was enough for her and as soon as she could, she would rid herself of these unseemly rags. Her departure from the orphanage was swift. Sister Catherine walked her to the main gates and said her farewell. She was sad to see Sally leave but at the same time thankful that she was able to escape the brutal hardship that went on within the walls of the orphanage.

The Submissive Scullery Maid
Shiralyn J. Lee

"Goodbye, Sally McGuire. I will surely miss having you around here. Keep well, young lady," Sister Catherine called out with a heavy heart as Sally walked through the gates and away from the grounds.

A thick blanket of fog had formed over the city and before long it was difficult to see in front of her. Sally waited a little way down the road for her friend to show up, just as she had promised. She sat on a small brick wall that edged the front of a terraced house and listened out for any sounds of her friend approaching. She was cold and her clothes had become dampened by the moisture in the misty cloud but she wasn't going to move from this important spot.

A short while later Sally could hear muffled voices in the distance. They were females and something had made them giggle. She listened intently to see if she could recognise her friend's voice.

"Eveleen, is that you?" Sally spoke nervously. She stood up hesitantly and tried to stare through the misty damp air.

"Sally, I'm here, I've come to take you away," a light-hearted reply came forth.

Eveleen slowly emerged through the white cloud and her excitement at seeing Sally free and ready to go with her was just too overwhelming. There was laughter and tears and hugs followed by more laughter.

She introduced her companion to Sally. Abigail, a cousin of hers who had been waiting for Eveleen to join her on her travels when she was free from the orphanage. They had made a pact as young children that they would travel to England and settle in London where they would make their fortunes in the city.

"Are ya with us, Sally? Please say yes, say that you'll come and besides, what have ya got to lose?" Eveleen pleaded with her friend.

The Submissive Scullery Maid
Shiralyn J. Lee

How could Sally say no to her adorable friend? There was no time like the present to make vast decisions like these. Sally nodded her head yes. "But how am I goin' to pay my way?"

"I have enough money. At least enough to take the three of us across the Irish Sea and into Liverpool. From there we can travel down to London and find work." Abigail said as she put her hand into a hidden pocket in her skirt and pulled out a fair amount of coins.

Sally's eyes widened. She'd never seen that much money before. "How did you get it, that must have taken you a hell of a long time to save that?"

"Are ya not playin' with a full deck? Saving? Let's just say that I didn't have to do too much. I was on my back for most of it," she informed her.

"She's no eejit, Abigail. I have some bread for you Sally, eat up 'cos we must make our way to the port. No time like the present to make our dreams come true, is there," Eveleen pointed out.

Through the dense fog they made their way to the port on foot but Sally had asked for a detour before they left. She needed to take one final look at the house that she and her mother had tried to call home. It seemed as though that was a lifetime ago and her memories had become distorted. They walked down Kildare Street and Sally could feel her childhood recollections flooding through her mind. Her tears came easily when she stood outside the building and looked up at the third floor. She pointed up to the tiny widow and told the girls all about her mother and how she had given her soul to make sure that her only child could survive. Eveleen hugged her friend and began to get emotional herself. It brought back her own memories of when she had lost her own mother. She too had been in a similar position to Sally, where her father had left them many years ago but unlike Sally, she had had the support of her aunt when her mother fell ill from cholera and died. But it wasn't too long before her aunt fell ill from the same fatal disease and passed away, leaving her alone with her uncle. He

17

had no time for small children and sent her to the orphanage and packed up his belongings and moved to London himself. This is where Abigail got the idea from and a pact was made before she had to say goodbye to her favourite cousin. Her mother was Eveleen's other aunt but she had no means to take in the child and bring her up as her own. She had regretted this until the day she passed away herself. Abigail and Eveleen always knew that if she had found the resources, she would have pulled Eveleen out of the orphanage immediately.

"Tis time to be movin' on. We need to make it to Liverpool before nightfall," Abigail told them.

The port was a noisy place to be. Sailors were practically running off one ship as they had just landed and were desperate for two things, Whisky and women. Other ships were either being loaded or unloaded and large sacks of sugar and tea were carried by workers to and from the warehouses that surrounded the port. The seagulls flew low overhead and screeched loudly as they fought amongst themselves as they attempted to steal any crumbs of food that may be tossed to the ground. The air smelt extremely salty and a stench of dead fish also drifted through the harbour, causing Sally to feel a little sick.

"I'm sure that you'll feel fine soon, Sally," Eveleen assured her.

They boarded the boat and patiently waited for it to set sail. Sally stood on the deck, taking her last look and saying her final farewells to her beloved Ireland, as they moved away from the port and sailed out into the sea. She rested her arms on the side and looked down at the water beneath them. The crests of water hit the side of the boat, swirling around and almost sending her into a hypnotic state.

Eveleen and Abigail joined her and the three of them ate chunks of bread and sipped water from a hip flask that Eveleen had brought with her. Their plan was to buy some food once they reach land before travelling down to London. How they were going to do that had not yet been discussed.

The Submissive Scullery Maid
Shiralyn J. Lee

As the boat sailed further out it picked up speed, which gave the girls a feeling of excitement and new adventures. The fog had lifted and the clear sky was now turning to dusk—stars were beginning to twinkle and the half-crescent moon had replaced the fading sun. They would be landing at Liverpool docks fairly soon.

"Let's wait by the gate, I want us to be the first Irish girls to leave the boat," Abigail said. She was eager to put her feet on English soil and it couldn't come soon enough.

They waited closely to the exit gate and when the boat had been safely moored to the dock, Abigail grabbed Sally and Eveleen and almost dragged them in front of everyone else. They were the first to step on to English land and Abigail just let out all of her emotions. She raised her arms in the air and danced around the other two girls, singing and skipping and thanking god that they made it safely in one piece. "My friends, we're just a hop skip and a jump away from our destination. I can smell London from here. It's filled with hopes and promises and everything that we all dreamt of, maybe a rich fella too."

Sally and Eveleen watched their friend in her merriment and joined in the dancing. They held hands and twirled around in a circle, getting dizzy with excitement.

"Stop, stop, I can't dance anymore," Sally yelled, but she was still enjoying the moment.

The three girls were exhausted but had found their second wind and within minutes they had left the harbour and were making their way through the streets of Liverpool. A woman stood on the corner of a street and told them to clear off, as this was her patch. Sally was confused by her outburst but Abigail knew what she was complaining about. And that meant that if she was getting paid for her services, then this was where Abigail was going to offer hers.

"You two go and wait in that pub over there. Here's a couple of shillings to buy ya-selves some drinks and a bite to eat. I'll be back with more money before ya know it." Abigail backtracked to where they had just seen the gobby cow and stood on the corner opposite her. She was prettier than the woman and although her dress was plain and simple, her beauty far outweighed that of a fat harlot in a piece of red fluff that she'd wrapped around her shoulders in an attempt to make her look attractive and alluring.

"I thought that I told you to clear off. You better not be trying to steal my money from me. I stand here every night to earn a few shillings for my whisky," she protested loudly.

Abigail said nothing. Instead she tucked part of her skirt up to indicate her business to anyone passing by and waited. And when a likely gentleman came walking by she gathered the rest of her skirt and lifted it up to show him even more of her leg. She gave him a coy look to seduce him and before the gobby cow could complain, the gentleman had his arm looped into Abigail's and they disappeared down an alleyway and hid behind a wall.

"What a nice looking gal you are," he said to her and then stole a kiss from her as he backed her up to the brick wall, pressing his body up against her.

His hands worked fast as his lips kissed her chin and her neck and her now revealing chest. Her top buttons had been opened by his quick working fingers and now he had one hand up beneath her skirt. The cold night air showed their breath as they both panted heavily. It took a mere two minutes for him to enter her and do his business. After that, he threw a few shillings on the ground and Abigail grovelled on her knees to pick them up.

"You were better than that ugly fat cow over there. Maybe you'll get a few more gentlemen callers tonight and you'll be set to fill your purse." He walked away leaving Abigail to search for her coins in the dark shadows cast by the alley walls.

The Submissive Scullery Maid
Shiralyn J. Lee

She immediately got back up and brushed herself down, buttoned up her top but not all the way and then walked back to the corner to wait for any other gentleman who would be interested in her services. She totalled three more men after that. They couldn't last long when they fucked her, two of them were sailors fresh off a ship and the other was a strange man. He was silent and just gestured her to lie down on the cobblestones. He lifted her skirt and inspected her naked lower regions. She felt a little intimidated by him but he had paid her good money in advance and looked like a proper gentleman. He wore a black top hat and a cloak and had a walking cane with a brass horses head to hold on to. But the thing that Abigail found strange, was the fact that he didn't fuck her as a normal man would have, he instead used his fingers and parted her vagina lips and rubbed gently at first. Abigail began to feel at ease but then he would change his motion and became a little rough and inserted his fingers inside her. She was unnerved by him and still he remained silent. His actions changed once again and now he was more courteous and gentle and as he glided his thumb over her clitoris her legs began to twitch and her stomach convulsed but in a way that she began to enjoy. She closed her eyes and bit down hard on her lower lip to prevent herself from crying out with pure lust. His fingers were the work of a magic man and now lost in a world of seduction, Abigail experienced a sensation that she had never felt before. It was a taboo bodily act and no one had ever mentioned this to her before.

Her orgasm had sent her mind into thoughts of crazy and happy—at the same time, confusing her senses. She burst out into a fit of laughter, not to insult the man but because she understood that she had been missing out on something so wonderful and she possessed this without even knowing it. The man stood up, his structure towered over her and his shadow cast a black image on the wall behind him. He was almost frightening to Abigail and she began to pull her skirt back down her legs. He stopped her from doing this with his walking stick by stomping it between her legs. He then used the end of it to push the skirt back up to her waist, leaving her privates on show for him once again. She looked up at him in fear and wondered what he was playing at. Now she was the silent one and her fate lay in his hands. He knelt down in front of her, still holding his walking stick. His eyes glared directly at her, piercing and cold as if he wished she was dead. Abigail drew in a sharp breath thinking that this was it, that she was going to meet her maker any time now. But the man surprised her. Her touched the open flap on her bodice and lifted it to cover her bare breast. He then kissed his finger and pressed it on to her forehead and smiled. But the smile was not that of a kind act, it was cynical to Abigail and she wanted him gone fast. It was like he had just read her mind and taking one final look at her vagina, he stood back up, pulled his cloak around him, tipped his hat as a thank you and walked slowly away, tapping his walking stick on the cobblestones as he stepped over them.

That was enough for Abigail, she didn't even wait to tidy herself up. She just ran out of the alley way, past the fat harlot on the corner, who was by now mystified as to why Abigail was running half dressed. She buttoned her top up as her feet carried her far away from the area and into the safety of the pub where her two friends were waiting for her.

"Quick, give me ya whiskey," she panted and stole the drink right out of Eveleen's hand. She sat down and gulped another whiskey that Eveleen had ordered her earlier.

"What happened to you, why are you so scared?" Sally asked her.

"I have just experienced the most creepiest fella that I could ever wish to meet. Trust me, ya don't want to know."

"But, Abigail, maybe you should tell us what happened," Sally asked her, confused by all the commotion that she was creating.

"Shush, be quiet Sally. We don't want the likes of any policemen arresting us. Abigail did what she had to do and one day I shall repay her and with interest too. Because of Abigail's willingness, we can now travel to London on a train. Now drink up girl, you've been holding that glass in your hand for an hour now."

The Submissive Scullery Maid
Shiralyn J. Lee

"I'm sorry but I don't think that I can drink, Eveleen. It smells just awful," Sally said sneering her nose at the drink.

"Well I'll bloody-well drink it, then." Abigail snatched it from Sally's hand and swigged it down in one gulp. She wiped her mouth with the back of her hand, belched and encouraged the others to join her on the next step of their journey.

They left the comfort of the pub and headed to the train station. Whilst the other two remained unaware of Abigail's encounter, they were also unaware of how quickly she wanted to leave this city. This man had changed something inside her, he had awoken her lust and she couldn't deny that she wanted to experience this again but his mannerism had caused her to be concerned for her welfare. He was not normal and it was due to his creepy characteristic that she felt that they should all be as far away from this City as possible.

They stayed the rest of the night in the waiting room for the next train to arrive. Huddled together on a wooden bench, Sally had rested her head on Eveleen's shoulder and fallen asleep. Eveleen asked Abigail what she had encountered and she explained everything that this man had done to her. Eveleen was intrigued by the taboo act and pressed her friend for more information. Abigail went into great detail about it and even now, she found herself wanting this strange man to touch her there again.

The train whistle sounded off in the distance. Eveleen stroked Sally's face and nudged her shoulder to wake her up. "Come on, sleepy head. The train's here."

Sally opened her eyes and yawned. "Are we in London yet?"

"Jaysus, she's a bit dense at times," Abigail jested.

The Submissive Scullery Maid
Shiralyn J. Lee

Chapter Three

The train arrived at Euston Station later that night. The thrill of arriving at their destination couldn't be compared to anything any of the girls had ever felt before.

"We're here, we're finally here," Abigail stated with glee. Her jaw dropped at the sheer thought that they could now consider themselves at home.

"So where do we go from here, does anyone have any suggestions?" Sally asked.

"I'm going to find us a room for the night. It's a big city, I'm sure there'll be plenty to rent," Abigail informed them.

It was getting late and they had been walking for a while now. They stopped and asked a local prostitute where they could find a room for the night. At first she rudely told them sling their hook but after seeing how tired and frail the red haired girl looked compared to the other two, she soon changed her attitude and sent them to a house that she would use when she had enough coin to rent a room out herself.

Eveleen knocked on the door of house that looked like it would fall down at any given moment. It was a slum but for now they just needed somewhere to put their heads down and sleep.

It was not a night that any of the girls could say that they slept right through. Women could be heard coming and going at all hours, some were drunk and disorderly and others were just damn cold and angry, or hiding from their wife beating husbands. Either way, the noise was constant and the girls would have to pay even more money if they wanted to stay any longer.

"I have to find work today," Eveleen said as she lay on the bed just staring up at a moldy ceiling.

"I think we all should. I know I can rely on the old girlie charms and the gift of the gab with the gentlemen if I need to, but I really need to find a decent job with steady pay," Abigail whispered. She didn't want any of the other women to hear their conversation, just in case they got the same idea

"My clothes smell like mold and stinky sheets," Sally giggled.

Abigail and Eveleen joined in the laughter and were annoyed at the fact that a woman in the next room, who earlier had made a loud fuss on her entry, banged on the wall and yelled at them to keep their noise down.

"Bleedin' cheek," Sally laughed.

As soon as daylight hit, Mrs. Grimshaw, the landlady, came knocking on the bedroom doors and ordered the all of the women to vacate the house immediately. Sally felt weak, she hadn't eaten properly for two days and it was showing in her health.

"It will get better, I promise ya, Sally," Eveleen told her trying to keep her spirits up.

They went downstairs where Mrs. Grimshaw was yelling at everyone to either pay for the room again or leave now. She was not the sort of woman to mess with either. She grabbed one of the women by her collar and threw her out of the doorway, screaming at her to never return.

The Submissive Scullery Maid
Shiralyn J. Lee

"Okay, I think that we should all go our separate ways and meet back here later today. At least one of us has to find work," Abigail suggested to the other two.

Sally was afraid to be on her own. For the past three years she had been given direction and her lack of street knowledge meant that she could possibly fail at this. Abigail set off on her own. She walked off fast without even looking back. Eveleen decided to set off in the opposite direction and told Sally that she would do just fine by herself and that she just needed to have faith in herself.

Sally stood still as she watched her friend disappear around the corner, leaving her to fend for herself. She was at a loss and knew nothing about finding work. She began to walk slowly down the street with her head hung low. A young boy selling newspapers yelled out that a woman's body had been found and that she had been murdered. Sally paid no attention to what he was actually saying as she walked past him.

She had been walking for hours and now found herself back at the slum boarding house where she was to meet the others. She waited for quite some time before the other two came back and joined her.

"Okay, I have got some good news," Abigail said as she approached them. "I think I may have found your uncle." She looked directly at Eveleen.

"How could ya have possibly found him, we weren't even looking for him," Eveleen scorned her.

"I know but it was by pure accident that I came across him. I met a woman who, let's say is well known around here and when I mentioned him she said that she knew where he lived. He lives with a friend of hers, Elizabeth Stride."

They decided to head for the house and find out whether he really was her uncle. Eveleen grew nervous. All that she could think about was how eager he was to leave her and send her to the orphanage where anything could have happened to her. She was not ready for this.

Abigail knocked on the front door of the house and then stepped back on to the pavement where she waited with the others. A woman came to the door and asked them what the hell they wanted.

"I'm looking for my uncle and I was told by a friend of yours that he lived here," Eveleen said to her.

"You're not from round 'ere, are you, my lovelies. I 'ave a gift for knowing these sort of things," she said as she rubbed her dirty nose on the end of her sleeve.

"My uncle, is he here?" Eveleen interrupted her.

"Well who would that be? There's been plenty of men folk walk through these doors lately."

"His name is Finn, Finn O'Leary. Do you know him?"

Elizabeth looked angry at the mere mention of his name. She stepped out into the street, forcing the girls to step backwards.

"If I ever lay my eyes on that whiskey drinking scoundrel again it'll be too soon. And if you girls know what's good for you, you'll stay well away from him."

Eveleen burst out into tears. She had been reminded of her traumatic past and now it was all for nothing. She hated this man more than life itself.

"Ere, you don't need to go and cry on me now. Come inside, all of you, come inside. I have a piece of lovely cake that I can offer you. Made it myself this morning, I did."

The three girls sat down at the table. The chairs were wobbly and the table filthy but right now they were being offered food from a very kind lady and this was no time to have morals. The cake tasted stale, it was probably a few days old but nobody minded that Elizabeth had lied. She'd probably stolen it herself and passed it off as her own cooking. By the state of her house it didn't look as if she did much cooking or cleaning or anything for that matter.

"Thank you for the cake, Elizabeth, it was very kind of you to give it to us," Sally piped up.

"Where are you girls staying? You don't look the sorts to walk the streets at night."

"We don't know, maybe we'll go back to the slum house and rent a room again," Abigail suggested.

"Well I wouldn't fret about that too much. If you're willing to pay for a room for the night, then you pretty lovelies can pay me and sleep 'ere."

They decided that it would be just as beneficial to pay Elizabeth as it would to pay for a room in a house filled with strangers. At least here they would have a better chance at sleeping. Abigail paid the rent and within minutes Elizabeth had gone out of the door and made her merry way to her local public house, where she could have a few whiskeys with her prostitute friends.

It was the middle of the night and the girls were sleeping soundly. Even with the wind howling through the hallway and a few drunken sailors singing as they walked down the street in hopes of finding a prostitute, the girls slept right through it. That was until Elizabeth came home. She flung the front door open and slammed it behind her. She cursed and argued with herself over Eveleen's uncle, swearing that she would kill him if he ever came back. He was a good for nothing drunk who stole her money and forced her into prostitution just so that she could pay her rent.

The Submissive Scullery Maid
Shiralyn J. Lee

"Do you hear me? You slimy drunk," she yelled, right before passing out on the stairs.

She remained there until the morning and was disturbed when the three girls made their way down, stepping over her as they past her.

"Ere where are you all going? I thought that we could all go out down the pub and celebrate our new friendship, for old times' sake. What d'ya say, hey my lovelies?" Elizabeth asked them, surprised that they were so eager to leave her so soon.

"We have to find work, Elizabeth, or we'll be finding ourselves cast out into the fekkin' streets pretty soon," Eveleen told her.

"Now don't any of you be strangers, do you hear me. You can rely on your old aunt Elizabeth if you need me for a room for the night. After all, we are practically family now." She got up from the stairs and still holding on to a small bottle of whisky, she struggled to walk without holding on to the wall for support. "Your old aunt Elizabeth will look after you lovely girls," she chanted to herself as she walked out of the house and down the street.

Later that day the girls went searching again for any kind of work. Eveleen was the first to find employment. A local pub had a position going for a barmaid. Eveleen, having her beautiful looks, was given the job immediately and would be working six nights a week to entice the punters in. She was ecstatic. This was to be her first position.

Abigail didn't find work that day, nor did she the next. But Sally managed to find herself a post in a house working as a scullery maid for Mr. John Forbes and his sister Agatha. They had recently inherited the property from their father who had passed away and were looking for kitchen staff. Sally knew all too well how to work in a busy kitchen and if it meant that she had to start at the bottom position, then so be it. At least she would be earning a real wage and also have a roof over her head. The post included room and board, so she moved in later that day.

The Submissive Scullery Maid
Shiralyn J. Lee

Her contact with Eveleen and Abigail was rare from now on but when they were able to meet up, it would usually be in the pub that Eveleen worked in. Her employer encouraged her friends to come in when Eveleen was working as they were two beautiful girls and that would attract the male drinkers to come in and spend more money. Abigail played on this and cheekily arranged with the owner of the pub that if he gave her one free glass of whisky on each of her visits, that she would flirt with the customers and push them into buying her a drink, meaning that he would benefit from her confident audacity.

Sally felt sad for Abigail though. After almost three weeks she still hadn't found any real employment and had been forced to work the streets at night. Abigail was okay with that, as she was making just as much money, if not more, than her two friends were and the added bonus was that she didn't have to do too much physical work for it either. Abigail liked to attract the male attention and she was good at it after all.

Eveleen was good at her job too, she gave her customers just as much banter as they gave her and she was good at enticing them to part with their money and buy one more whisky for the road.

Sally was settling into her new position quite nicely. Her new employers paid the going rate of £40 a year and gave her a bed and that was all that she required in life. The kitchen staff weren't so obliging though. Mr. Brookes, who was in charge of running the kitchen, gave Sally a hard time. He had no patience for young girls who were just starting out in the industry and trusted no one. He saw her as a potential failure when she first came in to the house and absolutely nothing that she did had given him any reason to change his mind. Sally wasn't so bothered by his rude behavior, as she had suffered much worse at the hands of Sister Agnes. If he thought that he could intimidate her in that same way that she had, then he'd have a long hard road to travel down before he was able to the job fully. Sally began to turn her nose up at him whenever he walked passed her and a couple of the maids, Emma and Polly, would find this amusing when they saw her do it and sniggered when he wasn't looking.

As a rule, the scullery maid usually worked the hardest tasks on hand. Sally was no exception. She knew that she had earned her place in this house but Mr. Brookes had made sure that she stayed at the bottom of the working ladder.

"Miss. McGuire, I see that you have been rather slow with your duties today. Make sure that you are not in this position tomorrow. I would hate to have to mention it to Mr. Forbes," he said to her with determination to ruin her working reputation.

Sally just glanced quickly at him. He really wasn't worth the effort. And he'd even forgotten that tomorrow was her day off and she had already arranged to go and visit her friends in the afternoon.

"Eejit," she muttered to herself.

She finished off her duties a few minutes later than usual. It hadn't caused a problem, nor had it interfered with anyone's working schedule, so for that old bastard to throw it in her face, meant that he was searching for a reason to be rid of her. She was not going to be thrown out into the streets just because an old git couldn't handle intimidating her. She would show him though, on her next work day she would work twice as hard and complete all of her duties well within the requested hours and even have time to make him a cup of tea and serve it on a silver platter, holding it right under his hairy flared nostrils.

She went to her room and sat on her bed listening to rain hitting hard against the window pane. She thought of her friend Abigail and hoped that she was not walking the streets tonight in this weather. If only she could find some decent employment, Sally thought to herself.

The Submissive Scullery Maid
Shiralyn J. Lee

The following afternoon she joined Abigail and Eveleen in the pub. Eveleen was still working but managed to involve herself in the conversation as much as possible.

"Have ya found work yet, Abigail?" Sally asked her in hope.

"I don't need to look anymore. I've found a way to service the gentry callers and stay safe. There's a parlour, it's not known to those who don't pick up prostitutes but wealthy gentlemen frequent it. They'll pay a good price for a pretty girl like me, especially if I'm a clean dollymop according to my new best friend Lizzy."

"Be careful, Abigail. These men do not care for the likes of an Irish lass," Eveleen commented as she'd overheard the conversation.

"I'm on the lookout for a Dark Cully to fulfill my dreams. That's a rich man who wants me for my charm and beautiful looks and will pay a good penny for a girl like me. Lizzy told me that a few years ago one of Angelique's finer girls, a toffer they called her, well she had a Dark Cully and he paid for her good services. He took her away from all of this and married her. That's what Lizzy said anyway."

"You shouldn't believe everything that you hear, Abigail. I'm sure tis just made up lies to seduce you," Sally told her firmly.

"It's a bloody true story!" she quickly answered her friend back and was annoyed at the lack of faith in her.

"Ere, you two lovely ladies. I'll offer you tuppence for a few minutes of your good nature," a man said to them as he stood at the bar leering over them.

Sally was horrified that he would say such a thing to her but as she looked around, she could see that the pub was beginning to fill with punters and many of them were women, the type who were clanking for it and would give it up freely for a swift drink.

"What's the matter with you, do you have a ponce waiting somewhere to collect his money? I'll pay you now if it suits you," he smugly commented.

"You, Sir, hold a candle to the devil himself." Sally told him and immediately got up from her seat. She was angered by his rudeness and without hesitation she said her well wishes to her friends and left, heading for the safety of her lodgings.

The following morning Sally was up at the crack of dawn. Mr. Brookes had already started his working day and snubbed her when she walked into the kitchen. She chose to ignore his manner and carried on pouring herself a cup of tea from the tea-pot that had been freshly made and was keeping warm on the stove top.

"Just wait till later, ya fekkin' old bugger," she mumbled just loud enough that he would catch that she'd spoken out but not loud enough for him to hear what she had said.

Emma and Polly were next to come down stairs and join them for breakfast.

"I've found myself a nice gentleman friend, Mr. Brookes. He said he wants to marry me as well," Polly said proudly as she seated herself nicely next to Mr. Brookes who had taken his place at the head of the table.

"And when does he propose to do this deed, Miss. Smith?" Mr. Brookes asked her in a rather stiff manner.

"As soon as he finds work, he's been looking for a few weeks now but he has promised me that I'll have the most elegant wedding any young girl could ever wish for," she replied dreamily.

Mr. Brookes huffed and then sipped on his hot tea.

The Submissive Scullery Maid
Shiralyn J. Lee

"And what about you, Emma, have you found yourself courting yet?" he asked her mockingly.

"Not yet, Mr. Brookes. I hope to marry a nice boy one day but right now I hope to save enough money just so that I can start up my own business," Emma answered him.

Mr. Brookes almost spat his tea out but he was too perfect to do that. No woman, especially a young working girl who could hardly speak an elegant word in the Queen's language, was taken seriously when it came to matters of business. It was almost unheard of.

"And why do you have a problem with that, Mr. Brookes? I'm sure our beautiful Emma is quite capable of becoming a business woman," Sally scorned him with her quick wit.

"And what makes you the expert on such talk, Miss. McGuire? With an accent as strong as yours, I'm sure that you'll never amount to much in the working field. No, your sort will not make it much higher than a scullery maid." He sipped on his tea again. His eyes were focused on Sally as if he was waiting for a reaction to come flying right out of her mouth.

Sally maintained her dignity. She had her back to him as she buttered a piece of bread and coated it with a dollop of jam. She smiled to herself knowing that one day she would prove him wrong. She had been toying with the idea of saving her coins and investing them in a business of her own. She had learnt to sew whilst in the orphanage, and did a grand job of it too, and had practiced making garments out of old sheets that she would steal when she had been put on laundry duty. She would hide the clothing that she had made behind a wall in an old part of the grounds that no one had taken interest in. Catherine had given her a darning needle and some thread to practice with. It was their little secret.

"If only you knew, you pathetic spiteful old fool."

The Submissive Scullery Maid
Shiralyn J. Lee

"Hum, what was that you said, Miss. McGuire?" he quizzed, knowing that she had said something whimsical.

"This jam, is it gooseberry?" she asked looking directly at Emma and ignoring Mr. Brookes' request to know what words had actually left her lips.

Sally had ambition. She had started to save her wages and stashed whatever money that she could under her mattress. She had envisioned herself as a shop keeper. Her profession would be a seamstress and she'd be a damn good one too.

"I'm going to have the finest wedding dress around these parts. Any girl would be jealous of me when she sees me in it," Polly announced. She was even oblivious to the conversation going on around her and all that she was interested in was wedding talk.

"Polly, if you're serious about your dress, I would be more than happy to help you out with it. I'm pretty handy with a needle and thread and if you supply the material I'll do a grand job for you," Sally informed her.

Polly jumped up out of her chair and threw herself at Sally. She wrapped her arms around her and thanked her for being so kind to make such a suggestion.

"Now I'm going to make blooming sure that my Blacky gets a real job so that he can pay for my beautiful dress that Sally is going to make for me."

"Blacky, is that his name?" Sally asked her.

"Yes, everyone who knows him call him Blacky. His father was a blacksmith and his real name is Archie but he hates being called that. He says it reminds him too much of his father on accord that it was his father's name as well."

"Get him to try down at the docks. My brother found work there recently and he said that they still needed workers. He may be in luck," Emma told Polly.

"Why thank you, Polly. That's real kind of you. I'll tell him to go there when I next see him."

Mr. Brookes raised his eyebrow and huffed, astounded at the very thought of being out of work, let alone working in the docks. His beliefs were snobbish and outdated.

The Submissive Scullery Maid
Shiralyn J. Lee

Chapter Four

S ally had been on top of her chores today. She'd given Mr. Brookes a run for his money and was almost finished for the evening, well ahead of time. She boiled a pot of water and made a brew of tea and then poured some into Mr. Brookes' favourite china tea cup. She added a splash of milk and two spoons of sugar, just the way that he liked it. When he came walking in to the kitchen he checked his fob watch for the time and noticed that Sally had finished exceptionally early. Just as he was about to speak and order her to find something else to do until her shift finished, she picked up the cup and saucer and held it directly below his nose. The steam rose perfectly and disappeared up into his large gaping hairy nostrils.

"Tea, Mr. Brookes?" she asked defiantly and then a broad smile emerged across her face.

Mr. Brookes was bewildered by Sally's behavior and reluctantly accepted the tea from her. He took a sip from it, making a slurping sound as his lips touched the hot liquid. He politely placed the china cup down on to the table and using his hands, he brushed imaginary particles from his shoulders. Sally waited for her recognition— anything to say well-done lass.

"Miss. McGuire, I shall certainly have to teach you how to make a perfect cup of tea if you wish to continue working in this employment. You may be dismissed for the evening, thank you," he said with no emotion to his voice.

Sally walked past him, remaining silent. But when she had left the room she pretended to walk up the stairs and then hid behind the open door. She peeked through the gap between the door and the frame and watched his next move. He sat down at the head of the table and sipped on the tea again, only this time he made a yum noise and closed his eyes as though he was experiencing a nice mellow moment.

"Bleedin' typical," she whispered to herself as she watched him enjoy it.

The next morning Polly was in the kitchen singing Blacky's praises. He had found work down at the docks and it was all thanks to Emma.

"He will be earning £80 a year," Polly boasted, proud that her man was now among the working class. "I'll be the Belle of the Ball."

It took several months of saving before Polly had the money to pay for her wedding gown, and now she was going to give Sally the chance to make her a beautiful dress to wear for her wedding day. She gave her a list of requirements, some were a little beyond her financial ability, so she had to compromise on what was really important. And a week later, with the help of Blacky's wages, she had chosen the material that she wanted to use and gave it to Sally to work her magic.

When Sally produced the finished gown, Polly was practically in tears of joy when she tried it on. The ivory silk brocade suited her skin tone. It had a flat pleated neckline and a deep V at the waist with ornamental buttons covered in silk that ran in a column down the centre, and a full skirt that made the girl seem even tinier than she actually was.

"You should be a seamstress for a living, Sally McGuire, you really should," Polly sang as she constantly admired herself in the mirror.

There was a knock on the door and Emma came in to inform them both that they had been immediately summoned to the kitchen by Mr. Brookes.

The Submissive Scullery Maid
Shiralyn J. Lee

"Polly, you look absolutely beautiful. Sally, you have done a grand job," she said softly.

"What is it, Emma, why are we being summoned?" Polly asked her.

"I'm not sure but I don't think that it's good news." Emma lowered her eyes as if she knew what was happening but couldn't face telling them.

Mr. Brookes was standing in front of the stove when the three of them entered the kitchen. Polly stood by the doorway to avoid marking her beautiful gown. Heaven forbid that she should ruin it just because Mr. Brookes was so impatient.

"Miss. McGuire, Miss Baker, Miss Dobbs thank you for coming so promptly. I have some news for you and I'm afraid it may not be good," he said with his cold stone faced expression.

"What is it, Mr. Brookes? Please just tell us, you're scaring us," Polly blurted from the doorway.

"I have been informed by Mr. Forbes that he and Miss. Forbes shall be leaving this house. The property has been put on the market and Mr. Forbes has informed me that they will be returning to America. They cannot assure any of us that we will be employed by the new owners and we may all be forced to seek employment elsewhere."

"No, that can't happen. I don't want to leave, I shan't leave," Polly cried and ran off to her room.

"When should we expect to receive our notice from Mr. Forbes?" Emma asked him politely.

"It could very well be in the near future. We are all facing an unclear prospect in this house, so I might suggest that you ladies seek employment elsewhere as soon as you can."

The Submissive Scullery Maid
Shiralyn J. Lee

A few days later it was confirmed that the house had been sold and that the new owners had no need for the present staff to stay. Sally had to act fast. She refused to be at the mercy of the streets once again and began her quest to search for any positions available. But it was through her friend Abigail that she was to find her next employer. A man, Mr. Cox, had sought Abigail's services on a regular basis and during one of his visits he had happened to mention that he was hiring kitchen staff. Abigail told Sally that she would probably be seeing him at the parlour that evening, as he frequented there most nights. She would put in a good word for Sally and as far as she was concerned, she'd practically got the job already, if he knew what was good for him.

"Have you seen the headlines in the Star newspaper?" Eveleen asked Abigail when she came in to the pub for a swift drink on Sunday evening.

"Jaysus, you know I can't fekkin read, Eveleen. Tell me what it says," Abigail snapped at her cousin. It wasn't something that she enjoyed being reminded of.

"The police have found a second victim murdered. She was a prostitute, Annie Chapman and they found her in Hanbury Street in the early hours. Her throat was slashed," Eveleen read out loudly.

"Annie Chapman? Poor girl. She used to go drinking in the Ten Bells. I hear that the police are looking for The Leather Apron," she informed Eveleen.

"Now who might that be?" Eveleen asked her whilst she poured a whisky out for the man standing next to Abigail at the bar.

"He robs the girls' blind. If they don't pay up he'll beat 'em to within an inch of their lives, so I'm told. He wears a leather apron and one was found next to Mary Nichols murdered body. He goes drinking in the Princess Alice pub but I bet he won't dare show his fekkin face for a while now if he is a suspect," Abigail reported.

The Submissive Scullery Maid
Shiralyn J. Lee

"Just keep off the streets, Abigail. I don't want to be reading about your murder next, now do I?" Eveleen advised her.

Sally joined them a short while later and Abigail gave her a piece of paper with the address to Mr. Cox's house. She assured her that he was a kind man and that the only reason he visited her at the parlour was because he and his wife had some sort of understanding. They loved each other dearly but they had grown apart in matters of the bedroom, fortunately for Abigail. Sally was grateful and didn't waste any time in seeking employment within this household.

Sally, now eighteen, had been working for Mr. and Mrs. Cox for about five weeks. Her eagerness to please her new employers showed and she soon found herself being given a higher position and was now part of the housekeeping staff. Sally had grown fond of her employers. They were kind hearted and forever trying to help all of their staff stay out of financial trouble by paying them a decent wage. Sally had informed Mrs. Cox that she hoped to one day have a business of her own, she wanted to open up a dressmaking shop, one where she could provide the ladies with the latest fashions that were fluctuating from France and become a well-known establishment. Mrs. Cox adored her little dream and told her that she hoped that one day she would be living the life that she wanted. Sally's plan was to save her money for the next several years and then put a deposit on a small shop somewhere in the near vicinity.

Over the next few months Sally and Mrs. Cox formed a friendship and they would take walks in the park together on Sally's day off. Their conversations, consisting mainly of Sally's ambitions and Mrs. Cox's boredom, as they strolled around the flower beds embracing the soft fragrances that drifted into their nostrils. It was during one of these walks that Mrs. Cox asked Sally if she'd like to earn a little extra cash. All above board but she would have to keep it a secret from Mr. Cox. Sally was excited over this. She would be able to reach her dream a lot sooner now. The following Sunday, Sally's day off, Mrs.

Cox invited her to escort her to a house an hour away, set on the border of the city.

Sally woke early on her day off, excited that she was going to become the next entrepreneur. She dressed quickly and quietly set off down the back stairs, just as Mrs. Cox had asked her to. She opened the back door and made her way down the narrow pathway, picking a daffodil on her way and smelling its fragrance by wafting the flower beneath her nostrils every couple of seconds. She got five minutes down the lane when a horse and carriage approached her from behind. Inside the carriage was Mrs. Cox and another young lady, Sally didn't know who she was.

"Step inside, child," Mrs. Cox offered, holding out her hand for Sally to take.

Sally placed her palm into the offering hand and climbed up into the carriage, she sat opposite the two women with her back to the driver. Mrs. Cox told the driver to hurry, as they were running late. He whipped the reigns over the horses and off they went, with Sally not knowing what to expect. She found it funny that Mrs. Cox had called her child when she was just a mere few years younger than her employer.

"This is Cassandra, she is to be my guest for the day and please don't call me Mrs. Cox today. It will be a less formal job for you, Sally McGuire. You may call me Lidia if you like." She smiled sweetly at Sally and Cassandra smirked at her from the corner of her mouth, then looked out through the window as they passed by the corn fields.

Sally couldn't help but stare at Cassandra's beauty, her long jet black curly hair and her bright blue eyes caught Sally off guard, as if she had the power to send her into a deep trance-like state without even saying anything. They chatted politely with Cassandra asking Sally questions about her personal life and what goals she sought in her future. Sally felt comfortable with this line of questioning and was pleased to answer anything she asked and freely offered more information on top of that. The journey took just under an hour and the horse and carriage pulled up outside a three storey red brick house. There were two white columns standing on each side of the front door supporting a small porch and a large dark oak door with beautiful flowers hanging from baskets on either side. A wisteria with its dangling lavender blooms caressed the entire front of the building.

The driver got down and opened the carriage door, helping the ladies out, one by one. Lidia ordered him to come back for them no later than 7 p.m. that evening. They entered the house and Lidia showed Sally around and told her what her duties would be. She informed her that under no circumstances was she allowed to enter the two bedrooms on the second floor. They would be completely off limits to her and that she had to be clear on the instructions given. Sally nodded her head, confirming that she understood her orders.

"Well, now that we've got that out of the way, how about making us all a cup of tea, Sally?" Lidia asked politely as she ushered her guest into the drawing room.

Sally went into the kitchen and lit the stove, using the chopped wood that had been placed in a large basket at the side. Whilst she waited for the water to boil in a pot she stared out of the small window and admired the tiny garden with its pretty yellow and pink flowers and the deep red poppies. She made two cups of tea and placed some biscuits on a china tea plate and carried it all on a wooden tray into the drawing room. Lidia and Cassandra were seated on a long red sofa. Lidia had removed her shoes and her feet were up on the cushions with her toes touching Cassandra's fingers. Sally pretended that she hadn't seen Cassandra tickle Lidia's big toe and carried on with her duty serving the beverages to her employer and her friend.

"Oh, Sally, where's yours?" Lidia had failed to inform Sally that this was going to be different from her normal job. She was expected to keep the house nice but that would only take a small amount of her time up and Lidia had no intention of forcing her to work a seven day a week job. She was to pay her for her services as and when they would need to eat and to just tidy up here and there. She was not expected to do much, just be around for Lidia as a friend. Lidia got up and went to the kitchen, returning shortly with a hot cup of tea in her hand. She offered it to Sally and dumped two spoonfuls of sugar, stirring it before Sally could even tell her if she took sugar or not.

Cassandra giggled as she looked directly into Lidia's eyes. Her full red lips glistened as she licked her tongue over them, removing any residue of tea.

"So, Sally, we have to go upstairs for a while to attend to some business. Would you be a dear and just take care of things down here? You could even go and sit in the garden if you like, the weather's nice and I'm sure you'd enjoy listening to the birds sing?"

The two women got up. Lidia brushed her dress down and did a curtsy to Sally. Her corset pushed her chest up high, giving her a huge cleavage, Sally hadn't seen her dressed so provocatively before. Cassandra, standing behind Lidia, reminded her that they had urgent business to attend to and that she'd like to get started immediately. Lidia responded quickly to Cassandra and excused herself from the room. Cassandra followed her lead and they disappeared upstairs into one of the bedrooms that Sally had been banned from.

Sally busied herself washing up the cups and then made her way out into the garden. The scent drifted from the flowers where she sat on a bench, momentarily closing her eyes and just enjoying the peace. That was until she heard Lidia shouting in the bedroom. It startled Sally and for a second she didn't quite know what to do. She waited, listening for any sounds. Again Lidia shouted and Sally clearly heard the word, 'bitch.' Then the words, 'whore' and 'fuck' were used. Sally ran into the house and up the stairs. Breathless and scared, she sat on the top step and peered through the banister rails, watching the bedroom door.

The Submissive Scullery Maid
Shiralyn J. Lee

It was shut. There were no sounds of disruption but she waited, wondering what was going on in that room.

Just as she thought everything had settled down she heard a loud slap and one of the women screamed out. Sally rose to her feet immediately and ran to the door, placing her hand over the door knob, she hesitated for a second, her hand trembling with fear. She made the decision to open the door and put a stop to whatever it was that was going on. It was to her regret that she opened it to be faced with Cassandra naked and tied to one of the posts on the four-poster bed and Lidia on her knees in front of her friend and her fingers fucking her. Cassandra had been blindfolded and gagged, and her wrists tied behind her. Lidia looked directly at Sally, horrified that she'd been intruded upon, she snapped at Sally and told her to return downstairs. Sally removed herself from the room and quick paced it downstairs and into the drawing room, catching her breath as she sat waiting to be scolded for disobeying her employer. Surely she would lose her position for this.

She waited for over an hour listening to the torturous sounds coming from the room above her. She could hear Cassandra begging for mercy and Lidia telling her to beg harder and some sort of slapping sound going on. She breathed deep and heavy, gasping at every noise made. Her mind was racing, her thoughts in turmoil, and her insides awakening. Sally had been privy to a scene unknown to her before this day and as confused as she was, she wanted to see more.

The bedroom door opened and immediately slammed shut. Lidia was on her way downstairs and Sally was petrified that she was going to be ordered out of the house. As Lidia entered the room, dressed only in her red silk full length gloves, with matching corset and black fishnet stockings with red garters at the top of each thigh, she looked at Sally sternly. "Do you feel foolish, Sally? Do you think that you should have respected my wishes and not strayed beyond the boundaries that were requested of you?" She placed her hands on her hips and walked in front of Sally, staring straight down at her.

"Yes. I feel very foolish, Lidia. I'm so sorry for intruding like that, I didn't mean to." Sally began to cry, her cheeks reddened and her mouth quivered as the tears flowed.

"This is how I will dress when I'm here, Sally, I like to parade naked most of the time but I thought that you had had enough drama for one day. Don't worry, I'm not going to banish you from my services, I need you. I need this to stay our little secret. You must tell no one, not even Mr. Cox."

"Thank you, Mrs. Cox, I mean, Lidia. I'm very grateful and I promise that I will keep this a secret." She wiped her eyes dry with the top layer of her skirt and managed a slight smile.

Lidia knelt down in front of her and clasped her hands over Sally's lap. She sympathised with the girl and understood that she was in shock after witnessing two women being abusive and sexually connected. It must have been an eye opening experience.

"This is consensual sex. Cassandra has needs just as I do and we release our tensions when the urge takes us. We are no more whores than we are lovers. It's a relationship unlike no other. Now I must return to my girl, she's a little busy trying to untie herself." She kissed Sally on her forehead and returned to her waiting subject.

Sally drew in a deep breath, unsure of what she had just agreed to but thankful enough that she still had her job. The sound of Cassandra's crying and Lidia's commands went on for another hour and then silence fell upon the house. The bedroom door was opened once again and Sally could hear them both walking down the stairs. As they entered the room Sally was faced with a new ordeal.

"Go and sit at Sally's feet, slut," Lidia said to Cassandra. She had tied a rope around her neck and paraded her in front of Sally half-naked. Cassandra's head was bowed low and she immediately went and sat at Sally's feet.

The Submissive Scullery Maid
Shiralyn J. Lee

"I don't understand," Sally told them, almost pushing Cassandra away from her.

"Shush now, Sally, be quiet, you're Cassandra's special guest. Bitch, lick her feet," Lidia snapped.

Cassandra lifted Sally's foot and removed her shoe. She caressed the sole with the palm of her hand and began to suck on Sally's toe. Sally pulled her foot away immediately and stood up— horrified that such a performance was being carried out in front of her.

"I can't do this," she said and stormed off to the kitchen, shocked that Lidia had even had the audacity to think that she would be okay with this.

Lidia had expected this from Sally but she still insisted that Cassandra was the one to blame for Sally's quick exit. She slapped her across her buttocks several times, leaving red hand prints on her bare skin.

Sally stood by the sink and stared out of the window; even though she was trembling she could still feel the sensation of Cassandra's warm mouth on her toe. She unwittingly liked it but refused to admit to herself that this was a good thing.

Lidia carried on parading a half-naked Cassandra around the house for the rest of the afternoon, keeping the girl on her hands and knees to humiliate her in front of the help. Cassandra liked her treatment, how Lidia ridiculed her to Sally and forced her to perform sexual acts openly with a chance that she might be caught by their servant. Lidia forced her to lie on her back on a rug in front of the fireplace, her legs wide open, she was ordered to play with herself until given permission to stop. She told her to continue at this pace but under no circumstances was she allowed to experience full pleasure.

"Think of my tongue on you, licking you slowly and playing with you. Umm my soft wet warm tongue wants to make my horny slut come." She licked her lips salaciously, teasing her little slave girl. "Make yourself come," she whispered wickedly.

Cassandra built herself up, fingering her clit in circular motions. Her breathing deepened, her eyes rolled back, she was on the verge of coming.

"Stop! You little whore!" Lidia shouted. "I don't think you deserve to come. Crawl over here to me."

Cassandra crawled over to Lidia who was now seated on the red velvet couch. She was sexually frustrated and needed to release her frustrations but her mistress knew best. Sally found herself becoming intrigued by two women having intercourse and sneaked out into the hallway, steadying herself by the gap between the door and the wall, watching the sex show as it graduated to the next level.

Lidia stood up before her slave. Her breasts bursting over the top of the corset as she turned around and knelt on the couch, her knees dug into the cushions and her body stretched over the back as she wiggled her butt in front the girl.

"You know what to do, my little whore." She put one of her hands on her buttock and pulled it, parting her cheeks to enable her slave girl to bury her face.

As Cassandra planted her face into Lidia's crevice, Sally gasped loudly and then slapped her hand over her mouth to control the sound. She picked up her skirt and petticoat and hurried into the kitchen and out through the back door, breathing in the air intensely. Images of the two women took over her thoughts. She couldn't understand why she was drawn to their sadistic act.

She remained in the garden until Lidia called out to her later that afternoon. It was time for the women to leave and return back to the City house. Sally tidied the drawing room and washed the tea cups that she had left in the sink and then joined the other two ready to leave.

The Submissive Scullery Maid
Shiralyn J. Lee

"Sally, I do hope you haven't been disturbed by our behaviour today," Cassandra asked her now that she was back to her normal self.

"Oh no, I'm quite fine." She waved her hand in front of her face as if she were saying that she'd dismissed the whole thing ages ago, but secretly she couldn't get it out of her mind. Without realising it, she had been turned on by her visions.

"Well then, that's all right, shall we make a move?" Lidia interrupted. She came across as a little callous in Sally's mind but realistically she too had experienced something when she'd seen the look in Sally's eyes whilst they'd entertained themselves.

The three women entered the carriage that awaited them and the journey home was a lot quieter than it had been on the way. Sally once again sat with her back to the driver whilst the other two sat next to each other, sharing a look between them that Sally could only interpret as true love. She was fascinated with how they had interacted with each other, how Cassandra had allowed Lidia to humiliate and control her so aggressively in front of a practical stranger. She couldn't help but think what type of game play was this and why did she feel so attracted to it? Every time that she thought about their sexual acts she became secretly aroused and had to keep looking out of the window so the others wouldn't catch her blushing.

The carriage pulled half way up the driveway and Lidia, now Mrs. Cox, let Sally out to walk the rest of the way back to her quarters. Sally stepped onto the gravelled pathway and said her goodbye to Cassandra. Mrs. Cox told her that she would see her tomorrow morning and her parting words to Sally were to keep today top secret.

Sally walked along the pathway and stopped to stare at a herd of cattle in a field. She leant on the wooden fence and began to daydream about being touched between her legs, kissed on her neck and spanked on her buttocks. She thought about Mrs. Cox and her ability to control another person the way that she did. Sally wanted to know more and

51

decided that she would delve deeper into this secret life and take on the practice being obedient for her mistress.

The next morning she woke early, ate her breakfast and began her household duties. Mr. Cox was in the dining room sitting at the head of the table, reading the morning news paper and slurping on his coffee.

"Good morning, Sally. My, you're looking flushed this morning, is everything all right with you?" he asked as he watched her bring in a second place setting for his wife.

"Yes, Mr. Cox, and thank you for asking," she quickly remarked— her cheek colour caused by her notion to keep her dirty little secret a secret from him. She was thankful that he couldn't read her mind, or he'd probably keel over with a heart attack if he could.

He asked her to pour him a second cup of coffee just as Mrs. Cox walked into the room. She was graceful and beautiful, her long brown curly hair bounced as she paced toward her seat at the other end of the table.

"So I see that Jack the Ripper has struck again," Mr. Cox mentioned nonchalantly as he folded his paper and placed it on the table. "But don't fear, ladies, it seems as though he's just murdering prostitutes."

"John, please! I think this is a serious matter, even if the murderer has concentrated on one area," Mrs. Cox retorted—her tone none too pleased with her husband's comments.

Sally kept her opinions to herself knowing that these poor girls, who were just trying to earn a living, must fear for their lives each time they went with a stranger. She too could have fallen into this trap if she hadn't have gotten this job. Abigail could have easily found herself in this way of life too and as far as Sally was concerned, she was teetering on the edge and could still find herself there one day.

The Submissive Scullery Maid
Shiralyn J. Lee

Mrs. Cox sipped on her tea and ate two bites of toast. She didn't have too much of an appetite after thinking about those poor girls being murdered by the hands of a maniac.

"Oh, Sally, I forgot to thank you for keeping my wife company yesterday. She told me that you'd been such an asset to her." He smiled at Sally and then winked at his wife, who in return bowed her head graciously in acknowledgement.

Sally, embarrassed by his comment, could only think about what she'd seen and heard. How Cassandra had given herself to this sweet delicate woman that now sat at the table. But she wasn't so sweet and delicate as Sally had found out. She looked directly into Lidia's eyes, searching for any signs of guilt, any emotion that was just about to burst out and finally confess to her husband that she too was a whore. But somehow she had managed to maintain her dignity and portray the illusion that she was a devoted wife.

"Yes, Sally. I told my husband how Aunt Emma had taken to you. You know, when she said she'd make you a special cake next time we visited." Lidia had a look about her as if she was squirming in her seat waiting for Sally's account of the day. She'd be in a hot seat if Sally reported back to Mr. Cox where she really was yesterday.

"Yes, she did take quite a liking to me, I suppose," Sally lied outright.

Mrs. Cox smiled coyly at Sally and then picked up her white china cup from its saucer and sipped on her hot tea. She had coaxed Sally into her first lie and covered up her dirty little secret. Lidia knew that she would be able to trust her confidant now.

Mr. Cox drummed his fingers on the edge of the table and then pulled his pocket watch from his top pocket and checked the time. "Well, my dear, I'm sorry to have to say..."

"...Say what?" Lidia jumped down his throat.

The Submissive Scullery Maid
Shiralyn J. Lee

Sally was nervous that he had caught his wife out and wanted to play with her emotions.

"Please stay calm, my angel, I was just about to tell you that I have to leave town for a few days. Duty calls, you know." He pushed his chair back, got up and went to his wife's side. Kissing her on the top of her head, he told her that he would truly miss her whilst they were apart and that he wished that she could come with him on his journey.

"I'll miss you too, dear," she replied angelically. Her long eye lashes fluttering at him as he turned and left the room.

Sally began to pick up the china from the table and as she approached Mrs. Cox, her employer latched on to her wrist. She stared at Sally, looking deeply into her eyes. Sally almost dropped the precious pieces in the process.

"Oh my god, Sally, he believed us, you were very convincing." Lidia was excited that she'd managed to deceive her husband so easily.

The two sides of this woman were at opposite ends, one side being her innocent adoring love for her husband and portraying the best wife any man could ever wish to have. And then the other side, her ability to dominate and humiliate another human being, training them to follow her commands in an instance. Sally was drawn to the latter, she had been thinking constantly about how this had made her feel. She blushed, hoping that her thoughts weren't being read by Lidia.

"Will that be all, Mrs. Cox?" she asked politely. Mrs. Cox nodded yes and let go of her arm. Sally busily returned to the kitchen, taking the tray of china and left over food with her.

Mrs. Cox spent the day relaxing and writing out a few invites to a party that she and her husband had decided to hold. It was to celebrate their wedding anniversary. Four years had passed since they'd taken their wedding vows and they felt that it was a celebration that they wished to share with their closest family and friends. Cassandra was at the top of her invite list, if anyone was going to be there, it would be her. Once she'd finished writing them out she asked Sally if she wanted to take a walk with her to post them off.

Walking at a slow pace down the street, Lidia interlocked her arm around Sally's—they chatted politely between themselves. She held her white-lace parasol over them both to protect their milk white skin from the scorching sun.

After dropping the invites off at the post office, on their way back to the house, Lidia suggested that they walk through the park and visit the flower gardens. Her apt to portraying a delicate woman to her unsuspecting friends intrigued Sally, and how she had managed to deceive her husband all this time was mystifying.

They walked through the rose garden, pink and yellow petals filled the grounds and the scent drifting through the air seduced the women, so they sat on a small wooden bench enjoying the beauty that surrounded them.

"Mrs. Cox, can I ask you something?" Sally wanted desperately to know more about her employer's antics, she had been all too calm about the whole ordeal and Sally could hardly contain herself.

"Oh, Sally darling, if it's to do with yesterday then I'll make a suggestion to you now. We will talk at the house on your next day off. I'm sure you have many questions rolling around in that pretty little head of yours, don't you?" She looked deeply into Sally's eyes. She had such adoration toward the girl and she just knew that she had made the right decision to include Sally in her secret life.

They sat watching the world go by, or rather a young mother with her daughter singing rhymes as she danced around the flower beds. And a couple of older ladies commenting on certain varieties and that one of them had entered one of their garden roses in a local competition and came runner up. Sally smiled as she watched them, if only they knew that they had just walked past a whore and her companion, she thought.

Chapter Five

I t was now Sunday, Sally's day off, and once again it was arranged that she walk a little way down the lane and wait for Lidia. She waited for a few minutes just before she heard the horses trotting in the distance behind her. Her heart skipped a beat and she began to feel excited but not understanding the reasons why. The carriage pulled up alongside her and Lidia opened the door for her to climb aboard.

"So, Sally, are you ready for adventures?" Lidia asked with a beaming smile on her face.

Sally nodded yes. She wondered where Cassandra might possibly be and asked Lidia of her whereabouts. Lidia told her that she would be joining them later as she had been visiting an old friend and would be travelling directly from there. This gave Sally at least an hour of uninterrupted quality time on the journey.

"So you had a question for me, Sally. Do you still want to ask me?" She clasped her hands beneath her chin with her two forefingers pointed up towards her lower lip.

"I...I just wanted to know what it's like. What it's like being with a woman, I mean." She blushed and looked down at her skirt, playing with the creases as she tried to avoid any eye contact now that she'd asked the ultimate question.

"Oh, Sally, you do entertain me," Lidia giggled.

Sally felt a little stupid, she'd asked a sincere question, so she thought, and it didn't warrant being ridiculed. Lidia knew that she'd embarrassed her guest, so she leaned forward and patted Sally on her knee. Sally lifted her head and gave a half-smile. She'd already forgiven her for her mockery.

"So do you really want to know what it's like being with a woman, or being able to control her? I saw the look in your eyes last Sunday, you were embarrassed, I'll give you that, but I saw something else. Maybe my little maid has an interest in what I do." Her full red lips turned into a smile, she had captivated a small part of Sally's interest and now she was left wondering how to captivate the rest.

Sally didn't know how to answer the question. She'd seen and heard things that she never knew existed and her curious mind was just itching to find out more. But her innocent nature was holding her back, telling her that she'd better be ware.

"I want to know what it's like to feel a woman's touch—to have anyone's touch. I've never, you know, with anyone." Sally had embarrassed herself by admitting that she was still a virgin. She had been saving herself for the right person but had never found any boy to be interesting or attractive enough to want to.

"So how long were you at the orphanage?" Lidia had wanted to ask Sally the other day in the park but she felt as though it would have been an intrusion on such a lovely walk.

"I had just turned thirteen when my mother died. My father left us many years before that. Even though I was capable of looking after myself, they still shoved me in the orphanage. I think my father still lives in Ireland somewhere, we never heard a pip-squeak out of him since."

"Oh, Sally, I do love the way you speak. You have such innocence about your nature and as for your so called father, well it's his loss. I'm just so sorry that you had to go through such an awful process to get here." Lidia patted the seat next to her, offering Sally a place at her side. Sally moved over instantly. "I can show you what it's like to be kissed, that's if you want me to."

Sally's eyes widened as Lidia moved in closer. Her lips opened as they approached Sally's and her breath entered Sally's mouth. Sally's heart was beating fast, her head felt dizzy and she began to tremble. Lidia's soft red lips felt like velvet to Sally as she kissed her gently. Sally didn't move. She had no idea how to react to this situation. She stared into Lidia's closed eyes, her hand in mid-air not knowing where to place itself. Lidia pulled away, leaving Sally feeling awkward and foolish.

"Now how do you feel inside?" Lidia asked her as she stroked her face with the back of her hand, her touch light and sensual.

"I...I'm unsure. I think I feel dizzy," she replied. She ran her fingers over her own lips feeling where they had just experienced their kissed.

The carriage pulled up alongside the house and the driver opened the door to let the two ladies out. Lidia got out first, to be greeted by her waiting lover Cassandra. Sally caught a glimpse of them kissing as she stepped out from the carriage and thanked the driver. Lidia gave him his instructions and waved him goodbye, then she and Cassandra shared a moment of secrecy before entering the house. Lidia whispered something into her ear and Cassandra looked directly at Sally. Sally knew she'd just been informed that they'd shared a kiss and it made her feel as though this could cause some unwanted attention. Cassandra stepped back in favour of walking alongside Sally. She linked her arm into Sally's and they strolled together into the house.

The fire had already been lit by Lidia's part time housekeeper and a kettle of water had recently boiled on the stove. The house had a warm and cosy feel about it, even though it wasn't too cold outside. The inside of the house didn't get too much light with its small leaded windows and heavily draped burgundy velvet curtains. The logs crackled as they burned and the orange glow cast shadows across the room, giving an ambiance of desire and lust.

"What would you like me to do today, Lidia?" Sally suddenly asked. Cassandra laughed out loud and then whispered into her lover's ear.

"My sweet angel, if you only knew what images I have running through my mind right now."

Sally had understood her comment and gracefully left the room to make tea. She re-boiled the kettle and stirred three spoons of loose tea into a large china tea-pot. She placed the pot, sugar bowl, milk jug and three china cups on a wooden tray and carried it in to the drawing room where the others were waiting.

"Sally, come and sit in between us," Lidia instructed her in a friendly manner.

Sally sat on the couch in the middle of the two ladies and before she could pour any tea out, Lidia placed one of her hands on her knee. Cassandra placed her hand on Sally's other knee and the two stared at the girl with lustful eyes. Sally looked back and forth at them both, she was uncertain what they had intended for her and she tried to get up. Lidia held fast on to her leg and urged her to stay. She apologised for being so forward and realised that Sally wasn't ready for such a bold enticing move.

"What do you want from me?" Sally asked nervously.

"There's something that we'd like you to do for us but if you're uncomfortable with it, then we'll say no more about it. I'm speaking to you as Lidia and not as Mrs. Cox. We are really two different people when I'm here," Lidia spoke with an amorous tone.

"I'm not sure if I can," Sally quickly rebuffed.

"But you don't even know what she was going to ask you, Sally." Cassandra commented as she stood up in front of the two women. She turned around and removed her long jacket, then unbuttoned her white frilly blouse and slipped her arms out from it. She turned around and asked Sally to undo her laces at the back of her corset. Sally hesitated, not sure of where this was going, she placed her cup down onto the table behind Cassandra and got up from the couch.

"I will undo your laces, Cassandra, and then I will leave the room, if that's all right with you, Lidia?"

"I'm fine with that, Sally, you can go and enjoy the garden if you so wish," Lidia offered.

Sally took hold of the laces on Cassandra's corset and began to loosen them. She opened the back up so that Cassandra could step out of it. She wore a small white cotton camisole top with lace trimmed straps beneath it and Sally could clearly see her erect nipples showing through. Cassandra noted that her eyes had directed to her breasts, so she took it upon herself to bend in front of Sally, allowing her top to fall forwards and show off a little extra skin. She unbuttoned her skirt and dropped it to the ground. The lacing on her petticoat matched her camisole and Sally liked the quality. She admired the design and noted that when she gets her business up and running, that she would definitely make a similar set but probably make it a little more tailored to fit the body's structure.

Now that Cassandra was in her under garments Lidia took it upon herself to take charge of the situation. She reminded Sally that she was welcome to stay in the room but Sally declined and left, making her way out into the kitchen. The two women made their way upstairs leaving Sally to wonder what it was that two women do together.

Sally sat on the bench in the garden. The sun was shining down and she was thankful of the little bit of shade to protect her eyes from the glare. She loved the perfume that drifted from the roses and a hummingbird gracefully flew by her and sampled the nectar from the purple foxgloves. The birds were happily chirping, the bumble bees busy collecting from their favourite flowers and in the background she could hear the two ladies playing their sadistic game. She tried to dismiss it—her thoughts would drift into a poem she'd once read but she was constantly being reminded of the sounds in the room above her. Temptation was winning and her inquisitiveness was chanting in her mind to take note of what could possibly be going on. She had an idea how a man and a woman made love but how was it possible for two females? Cassandra's cries were getting more prominent and distracting Sally from her peace. She wanted to know more, to get a visual on their antics. But this was improper behaviour and a private matter between Cassandra and Lidia.

She sat for another five minutes, listening and imagining only what she could interpret what could possibly be happening. She remembered that she'd seen Lidia on her knees at Cassandra's feet with her fingers between her legs. What possible pleasures could Cassandra had gained from that? She needed to know more, something inside her belly was stirring, a feeling that she'd never experienced before but she liked it. Only when she heard the commotions coming from upstairs did she feel this and she wanted it to continue. She decided that she couldn't contain herself any further and went to investigate just exactly what was happening.

She crept slowly up the wooden staircase, being careful not to be heard by the unsuspecting two. She bit her lower lip hard to keep her from making any sort of sound as she sat on the top step with her head rested against the wooden spindles.

Lidia's voice was stern as she spoke to Cassandra. "Now get up from the floor and stand before me. Lick my face, do it better, damn you!"

Sally listened intently. She wanted to see what they were doing, so she crawled on her hands and knees to the bedroom door. Peering in through the keyhole, she managed to catch a glimpse of the two women. Both of them were totally naked and Sally gasped as she saw Lidia's elegant body. Her long slender legs and her pert breasts caught

The Submissive Scullery Maid
Shiralyn J. Lee

Sally's attention immediately. She pressed her face into the wood, trying not to catch her head on the doorknob.

"Get on the bed, on your hands and knees and wait for me like a good slut," Lidia commanded. Cassandra got on the bed and placed herself accordingly to her instructions. Lidia knelt down behind her and buried her face into Cassandra's backside.

Sally was shocked and looked away. She closed her eyes tightly, trying to dismiss the image. What possible purpose could this serve, she thought? She regained her composure and began to watch the show again. Lidia was now standing behind Cassandra with her hand raised high into the air. Cassandra's buttocks were her target. Her palm came down with a sharp sounding contact as she slapped the girl's cheeks. Cassandra didn't cry out, in fact, it looked to Sally as she had welcomed the blow and wanted more. She wiggled her buttocks in defiance to Lidia, which caused her to show anger towards her lover. Lidia called her a dirty little slut and then ran her fingers down Cassandra's back bone and down into the crease between her cheeks. Cassandra groaned as Lidia's fingers entered her, fucking her insides with a severe thrust, as a punishment for her insubordination.

As Sally watched, she was unaware that she was becoming aroused at the scene now in play. Her breathing became heavy, her chest pumping up and down and her mouth became dry as she carried on observing. She was getting wet between her legs, this was all new to her, she liked it, she liked the sensation that she was now experiencing. Her mind was confused but her body was enjoying its stimulation. She wanted to be there in the room with them. If only she'd allowed herself to take up Lidia's offer earlier, she too could be in there being touched by the silken skin of her employer.

Lidia fucked her lover with a passion. She insulted her at the same time as loving her and Sally began to want this. She watched for ages as the two women fornicated and tasted each other's bodies and without realising it, she had lifted her own skirts up above her thighs and placed her hand over her vagina. She was feeling herself in the moment of passion and the wet odour from her under garments had transferred onto her fingers. She quickly got up off her knees and in the process fell dizzy, catching onto the door handle as she collapsed back down to the ground. She made a loud thud noise as her body hit the floorboards, causing Lidia to stop what she was doing and go to the door. She found Sally in a heap on the ground and immediately saw to her. Cassandra had been tied to the bed, so she was incapable of lending a hand. Lidia dragged Sally into the room, calling her name to her to bring her back to consciousness.

"Sally, Sally, can you hear me?" she called as she tapped her on her face cheek.

Sally came to. She felt a little groggy and was unsure of what had just happened. "Oh, Mrs. Cox, I'm so sorry, I didn't mean to..."

Lidia interrupted her, "Please, Sally, it's Lidia and it's all right, you didn't do anything that you shouldn't have." She stroked Sally's forehead as she lay on her four poster bed with the pillows nicely plumped beneath her head.

Cassandra had wrapped a red silk robe around her and was casually propped on the other side of the bed. "You are a dark horse. I knew you liked what we were doing. I could tell the first time I saw you, the way that you looked at Lidia and then looked at me."

"I don't know what you mean by that remark," Sally quickly protested.

"Now you two, please get along, I don't want any squabbles in this house. We can all share and be free to be who we really are here," Lidia pointed out.

Cassandra's robe fell open, revealing her breast and nipple. Sally couldn't take her eyes off her vision and Cassandra liked to show off, so she allowed it to slip a little off her shoulder. She wanted Sally to see her naked body—to touch her. She wanted a fresh young virgin to touch her in places that she'd never touched before. Oh how she would tremble and be unsure but at the same time enjoy her new adventure. Lidia began to stroke Sally's neck and ran her fingers down over her shoulder. Sally didn't flinch. In fact, she watched Lidia's fingers as they glided over her skin and liked how she felt about it. Her eyes were now fixated into Lidia's as if she were under her spell. Lidia smiled down at her and ran her fingers over her arm and along the back of her hand. Sally reciprocated the touch and held on to Lidia's hand. She placed it on her breast, encouraging Lidia to feel her body. She wanted this to go further and pulled the bottom of her blouse from her skirt waistband. Lidia slid her hand beneath it and caressed Sally's skin with light touches as she made her way up toward her breast. Sally's breathing became intensified as she felt the warm palm reach her chest area. She wore no corset. A girl of Sally's position had no place in wearing such garments, which made it easier for Lidia to touch her flesh. Cassandra joined in and unbuttoned the front of the blouse, revealing Sally's camisole and a hand beneath it.

"Let me undress you," Cassandra offered.

Sally sat up and lifted her arms in the air, allowing her clothes to be lifted over her head. Lidia unbuttoned her skirt at the back and slid it down her legs. She was now topless and wearing only her petticoats and undergarment and her lace up boots. Lidia stopped Cassandra from touching Sally anymore and asked Sally to undress herself. Sally untied her boots and slung them on the ground. She stopped just for a second, realising that the other two had at least some form of clothing on and that she would be the only one naked.

"Your petticoats, remove them," Lidia told her.

Sally wriggled out of her petticoats and tossed them to the ground. All that was left was her undergarment and she could still feel that they were wet between her legs. Lidia tapped her on the top of her thigh, as a gesture to remove them. Sally pushed them down slowly, she was nervous and began to shake. Her bush was now on display as she slipped her feet out.

65

The Submissive Scullery Maid
Shiralyn J. Lee

"Someone wants to play, don't you?" Cassandra said teasingly.

"Well, Sally, do you?" Lidia asked.

Sally nodded her head yes to the question. She was too embarrassed to verbally admit that she wanted this.

"I want to hear you ask me to play with you, Sally. Tell me that you want me to play with you," Lidia said in a formal tone.

"I...I...I want you to play with me, Lidia," she said shamefully.

"That's better. Now I know that you really want it. I will make myself clear to you. When I ask you a question, you will answer it with words and you will end your answer with Madame, do you understand that, Sally?"

"Yes, I understand, Madame," she was quick to answer.

"Cassandra, open her legs wide and sit yourself between her thighs."

Cassandra acted immediately, she took Sally's ankles and spread her legs open, leaving Sally feeling extremely vulnerable.

"Now place your mouth on her and taste her for me." Cassandra leaned down and put her lips between Sally's inner thighs. She gave her one long slow lick. Sally jolted, she'd never been touched there in such a way and the sensation was surprisingly nice. "Taste her again and, Sally, do not move, I didn't give you permission to."

Cassandra tasted her again, sweeping her tongue over the wet pink folds and toying with Sally's clit. Sally's eyes rolled back. She licked her lips and arched her back. She wanted this, she wanted more. Her insides were in passionate turmoil and she began to rock her pelvic bone. Cassandra's mouth was buried into the thick bush but she didn't care, she liked the way that Sally's natural pubic hair parted in the middle, revealing a pale pink organ.

The Submissive Scullery Maid
Shiralyn J. Lee

"So you're a virgin? That means that you'll experience a little pain." Lidia told her this as she was still being licked. This was a ploy to distract her attention from the word pain, what woman wouldn't want to experience a little euphoric pain when they were having their parts licked? "Cassandra, stop eating her. Now, Sally, turn over and get on your hands and knees."

Sally turned and placed herself on her hands and knees, her legs slightly parted and her buttocks pointing toward the edge of the bed. Lidia instructed Cassandra to lie beneath her and to lick her in that position. She then instructed Sally to return the favour and lick Cassandra's parts. The two women began to moan and groan as they enjoyed each other's bodies. Lidia could see Cassandra's tongue licking on Sally's clit and knew that her next step was in order. She stood behind Sally at the edge of the bed. Running her fingers over Sally's pink folds to get them wet, she slowly slipped one inside her. Sally gasped at the pain that she now endured.

"Keep licking, Cassandra. Sally, let me take you to a place that you'll never want to return from," Lidia whispered to her horny slut.

Cassandra ran her hands over Sally's breasts, pinching her nipples to distract her vaginal pain. Lidia slipped her finger in and out slowly, it didn't go in very far but she knew that after a few sessions this would progress. Sally couldn't make out if she was feeling pleasure or pain, her senses were being confused by the two combined together.

There was a drop of blood on Lidia's finger indicating that she had just broken Sally in. She was no longer a virgin. Lidia carried on fucking her, gradually building up her speed now, as Sally was able to receive her thrusts. The three women all joined together in their orgy, lasted for several minutes until Cassandra came first. She cried out that she was having her orgasm, letting Madame know that Sally had done a good job. Lidia ordered her to remove herself from beneath Sally, so that they could both concentrate on their new toy. She ordered Sally to lie on her back and to keep her legs open. With Cassandra sucking on Sally's nipples, she put her finger over Sally's clit and rubbed it fast in circular motions. Sally's body jolted and she couldn't control herself. This experience was making her sweat, her mind was crazy with images of the two naked women and her insides were building up. She was confused, she couldn't breathe, she couldn't speak, her legs were trembling and she couldn't think straight, she arched her back and gripped the pillows tightly behind her head.

"Arrh...what...I...I...oh god...oh god...oh..." Sally had just experienced her first orgasm.

She laid still—her body spent. Lidia had just given her, her first lesson in BDSM.

Chapter Six

It was the day of the party, Mrs. Cox had busied herself with organising her staff and notifying them where she wanted everything. She oversaw the whole production as it progressed throughout the day. Sally had been instructed to take care of the decorations, she had a good eye for detail and her skills were far more superior on the matter than that of Mrs. Miles, the woman who had previously been hired to take care of that side of matters but she had disappointed Mrs. Cox that morning with her dreary old fashioned ideas of how she thought things should look. Sally did an amazing job. She decorated a long table with a white lace cloth and placed three large silver candelabras in the centre, and had the food surrounding them. Streamers ran along the high ceiling and flowers in tall vases decorated every shelf.

The first guests arrived. They were Cassandra and her husband, a man that she had been married to for five years. He was a tall boney man, bald headed and a moustache that curled up slightly at the ends. They were such a mismatch in Sally's opinion. Cassandra had to pretend that she didn't know Sally and passed her the fur coat that she was wearing. Sally took it to the closet and hung it up. She could smell Cassandra's perfume over it and checking to see if anyone was around, she rubbed the collar of the coat over her neck to infuse the perfume with her skin. She then greeted the rest of their guests and Mr. Cox, who had only returned from his business trip that morning, asked Sally to bring in the chilled Champagne that he'd provided.

Sally felt a slight twinge of guilt when she looked at Mr. Cox. She had had his wife's fingers inside her and allowed her to take her virginity. Yet Mrs. Cox carried on with life as normal when she was around him, as if nothing untoward had happened with her or Cassandra. He would probably dismiss her from his employment in an instant if he were to find out. Sally was now feeling a little vulnerable and wanted to disappear to her room.

"Oh, Sally, would you be a dear and hand out some of those delightful canapés that I had made," Mrs. Cox asked in her employer like manner.

Sally picked up the silver platters and offered the food to any guest that she encountered. Mrs. Cox had invited many well-to-do friends and Sally felt as though she was being looked down on. She knew that she was just a servant, a scullery maid, a whore but she still felt as though one day these people would be coming to her for her services and she would be choosing whether she wanted to have them as her customers.

A small orchestra had been hired and they began to play Mrs. Cox's favourite music. Mr. Cox invited her for the first dance and together they portrayed the couple who everyone else would be jealous of. Sally's heart hurt with jealousy as she watched the two of them dance in each other's arms. They appeared so in love, so adorable, so false! Sally couldn't watch anymore and removed herself from the room. She headed off to the kitchen, where she took a large bite of chicken and swigged on an open bottle of Champagne. One of the cooks caught her and told her she oughtn't to do that. Sally told her to mind her own business if she wanted to keep her job. She informed the girl that she could have her sacked in an instant if she didn't keep her mouth shut. As soon as she heard the words fly out of her mouth she felt terrible for saying them. This wasn't her character. It wasn't in her nature to be spiteful. She apologised to the girl, who by now had burst into tears from the harsh remark. Sally told her that she would never have her sacked and that she liked having her around. She told the girl that she had just received some bad news (a lie of course) and that she was remorseful for taking it out on such a sweet young thing. The girl, only sixteen, accepted Sally's apology and after wiping her tears away, carried on with her duties with tidying up the kitchen.

Sally, realising that she had momentarily changed into a monster, regained her composure and went back to her own duties as Mrs. Cox's chief servant. She pretended not to notice her lover touching her husband's shoulder, gently caressing it with a hint of love. And she also pretended not to notice how she would occasionally give him a light peck on the cheek, showing her adoration out in public. If Mrs. Cox wanted all to see how much in love she was, then she could have it. Sally would just have to be another one of her dirty little secrets.

The party went on until 2 a.m. and with everyone exhausted and drunk, it was time for them all to leave. Sally grabbed their coats, one by one, and helped the ladies put theirs on. She was tired and feeling slightly miserable but had to put on a brave face as the guests left the house. Mr. Cox was smoking a cigar and looked pleased with himself. He had just landed a great business deal that would probably make him and Mrs. Cox millionaires. Mrs. Cox was too intoxicated to care right now and asked Sally if she would be so kind as to take her to her bedroom. She and Mr. Cox didn't share the same rooms and so it looked as though he would be residing in his room at a much later time. He had just poured himself a whiskey to accompany his cigar smoking and Sally knew that he would be settled there for the next few hours.

"Oh, Sally, I do love the way that you touch me," Mrs. Cox giggled.

"Sally held her by wrapping one arm around her waist and linking her arm over her shoulder so that she could hold her hand. She guided Mrs. Cox up the winding staircase and into her room. Sitting her on the edge of her bed, she undressed her employer and put her in her nightgown. She had to be quick as Mrs. Cox kept slumping down in a sleepy manner and it made it harder for Sally to change her.

"Oh, Sally, I can't wait to touch you again. I want to fuck you and make you mine," she slurred.

The Submissive Scullery Maid
Shiralyn J. Lee

"Mrs. Cox, shush, you must be quiet. What if your husband hears you talk like that?" Sally replied calmly.

Mrs. Cox put her hand on Sally's backside and squeezed it. Sally pulled her hand away and told her to stop her antics. She liked what she was getting but didn't want the chance of being caught in the act, especially by Mr. Cox. She finally managed to get Mrs. Cox into bed and tucked her sheets in as she lay there sleeping off her unladylike drunkenness.

It was now 2.45 a.m. Sally had just taken herself off to bed, when she heard the sound of police whistles being blown. They came from different directions and she could hear the policemen shouting to each other that there's been another one. She opened her bedroom window and looked out into the street, it was raining heavily, making it hard for her to see but she managed to catch sight of one of them running into a neighbouring street and the whistles were still being blown. She could only imagine that they meant another murder had taken place. She felt a surge of cold run through her body at the mere thought of being seduced by such a hateful man that he had to kill women. Never mind them being prostitutes, they were still defenceless women trying to earn a few shillings to make ends meet. Sally closed the window and began to cry. It wasn't about whether she knew these women personally or not but they were her kind, the type that she had grown up with and confided in. She may well know at least one of them in mere passing but all the same, she had an indirect connection. She ended up crying herself to sleep.

She had only slept for a few hours when she was awoken by the rain hitting her window pane. She hurried to get up and once again looked out of the window but a silent street greeted her as no one in their right mind would have ventured out in this weather.

She helped cook in the kitchen and set the breakfast table for her employers. It was Mr. Cox who ventured downstairs first and he was looking slightly the worst for ware. Mrs. Cox joined him fifteen minutes later. There wasn't much conversation between them this morning. Mr. Cox opened up his paper and on the front page there it was. 'White Chapel Murderer Strikes Again!'

Mr. Cox read out the names of the two victims. "Elizabeth Stride and Catherine Eddowes have been murdered. Both were prostitutes and both were mutilated," he stated.

"Please, John, I beg you not to talk about such things. This is harrowing," Lidia stressed to her husband.

Sally stood silent. Her face had paled in complexion and she looked as though she was about to be sick.

"Please excuse me, Miss, I must leave the room at once." She practically ran out of the room and headed straight for the bathroom. She didn't even have time to shut the door and just made it to the toilet where she threw up. She collapsed over the toilet bowl and wretched again. Mrs. Cox ran after her to see if she was okay. Sally was as white as white could be.

"I'm so sorry, Mrs. Cox. I'll clean this up in a minute." She was stressed and Mrs. Cox could clearly see this.

"My dear, what's wrong, why are you so ill?"

"I know one of the victims. She was sort of an aunt of one of my friends. She made us cakes once, when we stayed there after just arriving from Ireland." Sally burst into tears, her eyes were red and snot dripped from her nose as she howled in distress. Mrs. Cox wrapped her arms around her and consoled her lover in private.

"Oh my poor darling, my poor angel." She held her tight, giving her a needed warm compassionate touch. "You must take the rest of the day off, I insist."

Sally sobbed into her arm, her tears marked Lidia's sleeve as she let it all out. She hadn't seen her friend in a while but she just knew that she would be in turmoil all the same. Sally couldn't face going to see

Eveleen, it would only intensify the sadness that she was going through.

Mrs. Cox ordered one of her employees to clean up the bathroom and she insisted that Sally remain in her bed for the duration of the day. Sally had no choice but to follow her lover's order and went directly to her room. She was there for about an hour, lying beneath the covers on her bed when Mrs. Cox knocked on her door and asked if she could come in. She entered with a tray consisting of a mug of hot tea, a roast beef sandwich and a slice of chocolate cake filled with a chocolate ice center. She lay the tray down at the foot of the bed and sat at Sally's side.

"I have discussed with Mr. Cox, and he also agrees with me, that I should give you a few days off from service. Now before you argue with me, I completely understand your circumstances financially, so I have decided that if I take you away to the house, we could pretend that you are working fulltime."

"But I couldn't take you away from here. I see how you are with Mr. Cox," Sally managed state.

"Mr. Cox is a good man, I am the last person who would ever intentionally want to hurt him but I have my reasons for being the way that I am, Sally." She picked the tray up and offered Sally the food that she had personally made for her.

Sally ate most of it. "Thank you, Mrs. Cox, for being so kind, I mean."

"I think I could let it slide if you were to call me Lidia, after all, we are alone up here," she giggled.

Sally smiled momentarily. Lidia had given her a reason to smile, she was going to spend some alone time with her.

"So what does Mr. Cox know about you going to the house?" Sally asked quietly.

The Submissive Scullery Maid
Shiralyn J. Lee

Lidia whispered back, "He doesn't know anything. I've kept the house a secret from him, it's in my grandfathers name and as far as he's concerned, I go and visit my Aunt on a Sunday and I take you as my travelling companion now. He has no clue about Cassandra."

"May I ask why Cassandra is married to such an ugly man, she is so beautiful and deserves someone handsome and nearer to her own age."

"Oh my sweet darling, she married that old boot because he can hardly get it up. No, the most she gets from him is a peck on the cheek. She had good reason for marrying him, now she doesn't have to make her headache an excuse not to make love as I often have to."

"You don't make love with Mr. Cox?" Sally was shocked at this revelation.

"Hardly ever. We are so close with our personalities but when it comes to matters of the bedroom, I tend to make all kinds of excuses. The thing is, when he tells me he's off on a business trip, I just so happen to know where he's really going."

"So he's not on a business trip, then?"

"Most definitely not. He has needs, just like I do and you, my sweet darling. But unlike me, he has to pay for it."

"Don't you hate that? The idea of him covered in another woman's scent."

"As I do, you mean? Now get some rest, we leave this afternoon."

Sally slept for three hours, her rest had helped her. Mrs. Cox had packed a few things for her to take and she waited whilst Sally got dressed and came down stairs ready to go. The carriage was waiting outside and Mr. Cox waved them off as they started on their way.

"Enjoy your vacation, ladies," he called after them.

The Submissive Scullery Maid
Shiralyn J. Lee

Lidia waved back, sticking her arm and head out of the window. Even though she had no sexual desire toward the man, she still held a fond heart for him and would surely miss his presence.

Chapter Seven

They were ten minutes away from reaching the house when all of a sudden the horses and carriage had to make a sudden sideways manoeuvre. It was here that a horse and black carriage went shooting past them in the opposite direction. Sally was frightened by the intensity of it all and held on to Lidia for dear life. The driver got down and opened the door, asking if they were all right. Lidia nodded yes and informed him to hurry to the house where they would feel much safer. He informed them that they had nothing to worry about and that they would be there in just a few minutes.

It was to the ladies relief that they were now in the safety of the house. The fire had been lit and the two women settled down with a well-deserved glass of red wine. Sally had never drank red wine before, so it tasted a little strange to her taste buds. She ended up having two glasses and became quite merry. Lidia was on her third glass and not far from being merry herself.

"Do you want to sleep with me tonight?" she asked Sally outright.

Sally almost spilled her drink. She could never have imagined sleeping with her, even though she had fucked her insides, she saw sleeping together as an intimate thing. Something one would do if they were married. But Lidia felt the need to be close to her, there was something between them, an instant attraction had grown into something deeper, something only they could know.

The Submissive Scullery Maid
Shiralyn J. Lee

"I've fallen in love with you, Sally McGuire. I knew the very first time that I laid eyes on you that I'd want to be with you. I kept my secret hidden well from you." Her eyes were wide, big pools of watery blue and her lips redder than ever.

Sally wanted to be kissed by them, she wanted her lover to take her in her arms and give her all the love that she could possibly share. Lidia had given Sally her most intimate desire, for the first time in her life, she was the one who felt submissive. Sally stroked her long dark hair, it was like silk to her, she stroked it again and this time Lidia moved in closer. She kissed Sally on her lips, lacing her tongue with her own. Sally responded by kissing her back and melted back into the couch as Lidia took control.

"What about Cassandra?" she asked, wondering if this was just a game to Lidia.

"We're lovers of an unusual kind. We met at an underground party, one that would turn your head, Sally," she said as she carried on kissing Sally's neck.

"What kind of party would that be, Lidia?"

"It's where men and women congress together and perform acts so disapproved by anyone who thinks that they're normal. Like us now, we'd be considered outcasts. I would probably lose my marriage, my home, my status, if anyone was to find out my hidden desires."

"I couldn't do that to you, Mrs. Cox. You've been so kind to me!" Sally cried out. She immediately got up from the couch and her emotions were running wild with her.

"Sally darling, please sit back down and talk with me. There's no need for panic right now."

Sally threw a couple of logs on the fire and gave it a poke. She sat back at Lidia's side and asked her what was going to happen with her and Cassandra. She didn't have a jealous bone in her but still needed to know where she fitted in this concept.

"Cassandra is my lover. She has been for a few years now. The bond we have is like no other. She allows me to control her, to humiliate her as you may well know. It's not love that we share but trust, I trust her with my life and she trusts me with hers."

Lidia placed her hand on Sally's lap, then let her fingers wander down the length of her skirt. She began to gather the material in her hand and hoisted it up over her knees. Sally remained poised, her inviting smile and glazed over eyes just said it all to Lidia. She planted a second kiss on Sally's lips, her mouth fully open and her tongue tasting Sally's as she seduced her. Sally ran her hands over Lidia's back and through her hair, messing it up as her fingers found their way around the strands. The two became one as their lips remained locked in their kiss and Sally began to feel aroused.

Lidia took her by her hand and coaxed her to follow her upstairs. As they reached the top step, she remembered that Lidia had told her to never enter two rooms.

"What's in the other room?" she asked her.

Lidia stopped dead and wondered if she dare show Sally her even darker secret. "Beyond that door is a world that you couldn't imagine. It's a place where only a few have experienced its power."

Sally had grown even more intrigued by Lidia's mysteriousness and wanted to know more. She urged Lidia to show her what waited her eyes behind the door and after gentle persuasion, she managed to get Lidia to agree to open the door. As she walked behind her lover, she became aware that it was no ordinary room. Lidia opened the curtains to let some light in and Sally gasped as she looked around.

"Do you keep prisoners here?" she asked, not sure of just what she was looking at.

The Submissive Scullery Maid
Shiralyn J. Lee

Chains adorned the walls on one side of the room, a wooden box type chair with leather straps attached to the arms and legs sat in the middle of the room and a wooden bench with a leather seat and more leather straps attached at the bottom on both sides.

"I torture people here," she proclaimed. "Sometimes they pay me and sometimes, as in the case of Cassandra, it's done under secret desire." She stroked the box chair with one finger and smiled as though she were reminiscing about something.

"How do you torture them and why?" Sally asked.

"You are far too inquisitive for an innocent girl," Lidia laughed. "Only those with true interest will know how this works, now let's get out of here and go to bed."

Sally's cheeks turned red as she could only imagine what went on. Lidia took her hand and led her into the other bedroom where she wanted to make love to her. They undressed slowly, Sally standing by the side of the bed and Lidia near the window. They both laid their clothes over the night chair as they removed each garment. Sally's clothes were simple but Lidia's underwear was more complex, she had to have the help of her lover to undo the back of her corset. This was a sensual moment as Sally loosened the ties that kept her lover restrained. The corset opened and Lidia stepped out of it, turning to face Sally, she told her that she loved her and Sally's heart mellowed at the mere thought that anyone could have such feelings for her. She lifted her camisole up over her head and dropped it to the ground. Her small pert breasts had Lidia's attention and as she slipped under the red silk bed sheets, Lidia quickly joined her.

Lidia lay on top of her, her hand finding its way down Sally's flat belly and in between her thighs. Sally opened her legs wider so that she could enjoy her lovers touch. She closed her eyes as she felt herself succumb to Lidia's gentle contact. Lidia played with Sally's clit, teasing it and forcing it to want more. She kissed and sucked on Sally's nipples, before moving slowly down her stomach, over her hips and down to her wet wanting vagina. She licked her pink folds, flicking her tongue over Sally's clit as she went from side to side. Sally writhed as she received the warm soft wet velvety touch from such a powerful tool. Lidia licked her slowly at first, caressing and seducing her lover, but then she changed her speed and began to lick vigorously, causing Sally to take in deeper breaths as she felt her insides needing to explode. Her legs twitched and her head lay firmly back into the pillow and as she gripped on tightly to the sheets, she released her orgasm into Lidia's mouth.

"I want to taste you," she told Lidia.

"I want you to taste me too," she replied. She straddled herself over Sally's body, her hair dangling down her back and her deep blue eyes watching her lover as she slipped further down the sheets between her thighs. Sally's mouth was now in direct contact with her lover's parts and she began to taste her for the first time. She licked once, unsure if she was doing it right, she waited for Lidia to complain. She licked again and still no complaint. Then she placed her entire mouth over Lidia's opening and began to lick and suck on the juicy flesh. Lidia towered over her, feeling her own breasts and pinching her nipples as she felt Sally's control take place. She rocked her body over her mouth, gaining her sexual desire as Sally teased her senses. She was turned on fully by this girl beneath her and within minutes, she came over Sally's face, jolting with each contraction as her orgasm was released.

The two women lay naked and spent on top of the bed sheets, Lidia had her legs wrapped around Sally's thighs and Sally's hand was rested over Lidia's breast.

"I don't know where we're going to go from here, Sally. I can't leave my husband for you, it's impossible for us to live as a couple." Lidia sounded stressed as she spoke and a tear made its way to the corner of her eye.

The Submissive Scullery Maid
Shiralyn J. Lee

"I understand, Lidia, I really do. You have to keep your social life the way that it is, and I will just have to stay in the background." She hated hearing herself say these words but she knew she was right.

They slept for three hours, the daylight disappeared and the pink night sky with a dusky orange was soon followed by the midnight blue and twinkling stars. Sally woke first, she felt fulfilled and satisfied. Lidia carried on sleeping, so Sally left her there, covering up her shoulders with the sheet. She crept out of the room as she flung a small silk robe around her. She closed the door—it creaked as it shut. Before she stepped any further, she had a sudden urge to investigate the room opposite again. Her curiosity had taken over and she didn't hesitate to open the door. The room was dark and cold, causing her to shudder but she still wanted to snoop. She sat in the box chair and placed her ankles into the leather restraints, her legs now opened wide, she realised just how intriguing this game could be.

Her robe fell open and her silky white skin showing, made her feel sexy and slutty. Shadows cast across the room and Sally began to feel comfortable in her situation. Lidia had woken and quietly opened her bedroom door without Sally realising. She stepped across the landing and watched Sally as she made herself comfortable in her chair.

"So you want to be my whore?" Lidia spoke seductively.

Sally jumped, "Yes. I want to give you total control over me."

"Then allow me to show you." She advanced forward into the room and walked behind Sally. Picking up a length of black material, she placed it over Sally's eyes and tied it into a knot at the back of her head. "You have begun your submission to me. I will not be as gentle with your body as before. This is a form of torture, slut." Lidia's voice had changed, she was stern with Sally.

She restrained her wrists onto the arms of the chair and opened up her robe. Sally was now vulnerable and at Lidia's mercy. She went down on her knees and began to nibble the insides of Sally's thighs;

The Submissive Scullery Maid
Shiralyn J. Lee

Sally bit her lower lip, anticipating her lover's next move. Lidia nibbled right up to her opening, causing Sally to gasp.

"Be quiet," Lidia told her.

She stood back up and yanked the robe down from Sally's shoulders, leaving her almost naked. She went over to a table and picked up a long finger of ginger root and with a small paring knife, she peeled it. Sally could hear the sound but was unsure what it was. Once peeled, Lidia held the root beneath Sally's nose, she didn't understand what she smelt but she liked it. Then Lidia parted her opening, holding her lips apart with one hand, she inserted the dildo shape of ginger with her other. Sally liked the way that it slipped inside her. At first she felt a warm tingling sensation, it felt good, but then the warm sensation began to have a harsher tingle, not uncomfortable but almost hot without it being hot. She began to fidget slightly as the ginger maintained its position. Lidia released her from her restraints and lifted her up from her seat. She held her by both of her hands and led her over to a wooden bench. Bending her over it, she restrained her ankles and wrists to the straps on each side. Sally's backside was in the air, she couldn't see a thing and her insides were beginning to burn.

"If you clench your cheeks, I promise you, you'll feel your insides burn even more than they are already."

Sally froze, unsure of what was happening, she heeded the warning. Lidia had a bamboo brush in each hand. They consisted of 70 lashes each and were 20inches in length. She knelt behind her subject and began to flog her cheeks. Sally cried out with the first thuddy sting, and Lidia asked her if she wanted to stop this now. Sally answered no. Lidia carried on with her flogging and knowing that it wasn't stinging her as a birch cane would, she gave both cheeks a swipe in unison, giving even impact on the skin. Sally's backside had reddened and satisfied with her work, Lidia released her lover from her confinement.

"Oh, I can hardly walk," she said as her red backside tingled.

The Submissive Scullery Maid
Shiralyn J. Lee

"Allow me to remove the root from you. This is known to us as figging," Lidia informed her. She put her hand between Sally's thighs, gently pulling out the object. Sally was grateful that it was being removed at this point.

"I did as you said, I didn't clench my bum," she said proudly. Lidia smiled at her for her willingness to learn something different.

"I was very gentle with you, Sally; I couldn't hurt you like I would a client or even Cassandra." She brushed her hand over Sally's face, feeling her soft cheek and rubbing her finger over her top lip. Sally bit down playfully on it. Her eyes were filled with a layer of tears as she felt emotionally bonded to the woman who had changed the course of her life.

Chapter Eight

T he next few days passed by quickly. Sally was able to distract herself from her friend's ordeal and with Lidia taking care of her personal needs, she felt wanted for the first time in her life.

It was time to leave and head back to the city life. Lidia was depressed that they had to leave the privacy and safety of their little love nest but she didn't want to cause suspicions with her husband.

The ride home was intense. She held Sally's hand tightly all the way. Sally made light of the situation and reminded Lidia that they would soon be able to be together on her next day off. Lidia was annoyed that they'd have to snatch time to be alone together and would have to think up a plan so that she could be with Sally a lot more.

They were a fast approaching the City now, the evening light had changed to dark and Lidia urged the driver to hurry as she hated being out at such a late time without a male escort for protection. The horses hooves sounded loud as they clipped the cobble stoned roads and the ladies could hear the driver whipping the reigns to get them to canter. Lidia had no reason for wanting to see her husband and for the first time, she was dreading having to be Mrs. Cox around him. Sally knew more about her in such a short time than he did their entire marriage. How was she going to hide her feelings from him? Her head was filled with too many questions and secrets and she wanted to just hide in her room until she could be with Sally once again.

"Are my eyes red?" she asked as she ran her finger under her lower eye lashes.

The Submissive Scullery Maid
Shiralyn J. Lee

"Here, let me clear that for you," Sally offered, and leaned in to kiss her eyes with a soft sensuous kiss.

The coach pulled up outside of the house. The driver helped them out and carried their bags to the front door. Upon entering the house, Lidia was greeted by her staff, there was an atmosphere as though something had happened but no one was telling. She asked Sally to make the most of her evening and spend it in her room reading or writing, or to just rest. Sally left her and made her way to her room. Lidia entered the lounge where a tall man sat waiting for her. He wore a tweed jacket and was smoking a pipe.

He stood up to greet her and introduced himself as Inspector Reed. He looked saddened and asked Lidia to sit down as he had some bad news to give her. He picked up a crystal glass from the sideboard and poured her out a large brandy. Lidia began to tremble—she demanded to know why he was in her house.

"I'm so sorry to have to inform you, Mrs. Cox, that your husband is dead." He paused and took a large swig of brandy himself. "He was killed three evenings ago. A black carriage hit him as he walked out of the Pig and Whistle pub."

Lidia fell back into her seat. She was shocked at hearing this news and couldn't believe it. The same night that she and Sally had left for the secret house, her husband was killed. She couldn't speak—couldn't think straight—couldn't breathe.

"Apparently the coach and horses were travelling at high speed through the streets. He died instantly at the scene. I have witnesses stating that they'd seen the coach approaching the City earlier that evening and it was in a hurry."

Lidia suddenly remembered that they too had come into contact with such a coach that evening, could it have possibly been the same one, she thought? She drank her brandy and lifted her glass up for a second. Her tears were being fought back as she listened to the Inspector. For all of his faults, she'd always considered him to be a good man, she was just sorry that she never found it in herself to love him in the way that he deserved. She felt remorseful for lying to him, for cheating on him with other women. She wanted to scream and let her emotions out but the Inspector's sympathy kept her from releasing it.

Sally had been told by one of the girls what had been going on and she too felt tremendous guilt for her actions.

"They say it was Jack the Ripper's coach what killed him," Lilly the cook told her.

Sally wanted to be at her lover's side to comfort her, but she knew that she had to remain loyal to Mr. Cox's memory, as she was living in his house, even if he was dead.

That night Lidia cried herself to sleep but she was soon pacing the length of her bedroom floor, her anger and feeling insecure had kicked in. She couldn't take it anymore and went down stairs to the kitchen, poured herself a glass of water and just stood staring aimlessly at the walls. Her eyes were swollen—her chin quivering. She had no idea that she was even there until Sally came down and spoke softly to her.

"Lidia, I'm so sorry, I don't know what to say to make you feel better and I don't think that I could. Please come and sit down." She noted that her lover was shivering, so she wrapped a tea towel around her shoulders and rubbed the sides of her arms. Lidia's head just rested against Sally's belly as Sally tried her best to comfort her.

"I feel shame," she mumbled.

"You've got nothing to be ashamed of, you're a wonderful person," Sally replied back.

"I feel shame not because I cheated behind his back. I feel shame because I didn't love him, because I didn't want to come home to him tonight. I wanted to be with you, I wanted to tell him that I wanted to be with you." She broke down and cried into Sally's stomach, her tears soaking her lover's night gown.

Sally could only be there for her in mind. She dare not show her affection for Lidia in this house, not where prying eyes could catch them out and destroy Lidia's reputation. She guided her employer back to her bedroom, her arm wrapped around the tiny waist and her shoulder supporting her body weight as they slowly made their way upstairs.

Sally put Lidia to bed, her gentleness went unnoticed but Sally didn't care, she could see that Lidia was distraught and left her to sleep as much as she possibly could.

As morning arrived, Sally went straight to the dining room as usual, not seeing Mr. Cox sitting in his chair and reading his newspaper was upsetting. She hadn't even considered herself as the other woman up until this very moment, it hit her hard, her stomach was turning and she began to feel sick.

Lidia entered the room. She looked tired and scared and walking past her husband's seat, she stroked the back of it and let out a huge sigh.

"I miss him, Sally." Her eyes darted toward the floor, she felt as though she was being torn inside. She couldn't be there for Sally right now and she felt guilty for that.

"I know, Mrs. Cox," Sally said compassionately. She guided her employer to her seat and set her place on the table. Lidia put her hand on top of Sally's as she laid her cutlery in front of her.

"Help me get through this," she whispered.

Sally nodded and poured her tea into her favourite china cup. Lidia couldn't eat, she just stared at the food on her plate and moved it around with her fork. Sally tried to convince her to at least take a bite to keep her strength up. Lidia nibbled on a piece of bacon. She chewed it for ages, hardly able to swallow.

Chapter Nine

The day of the funeral had arrived. Lidia, dressed in a black silk dress edged with black lace and holding on to a black lace parasol, stepped out of the house holding on to Cassandra's arm. Sally watched them as they set off and a small pang of jealousy struck across her heart. She knew she had nothing to worry about, Cassandra was part of the game but she felt enormously lost as Lidia hadn't been able to pay her any attention over the last few days. She wanted to be the one holding on to her arm and taking care of her needs. The realisation of her place in life hurt her, as she understood that Lidia would never be able to recognise her feelings out in public.

It was raining hard today and the police presence was strong, as another prostitute had been found murdered in her home. Mary Jane Kelly, a good looking girl who liked to sing. It was a bitter reminder as to why Mr. Cox had met with his death and the aunt of Sally's friend.

Lidia stood at her husband's graveside with her closest family and friends at her side. She felt faint, the rain poured down on them as they said their prayers and all she wanted to do was curl up in her bed and cry. She longed for Sally to be with her, she'd been distant and not paid too much attention to her lover. Sally hadn't complained, or even mentioned their private goings on. Lidia began to think about her, how her long slender legs, smooth and silky as they were, just turned her on. She wanted to kiss those pert breasts and began to imagine Sally's legs wrapped around her own as they kissed. It was as though her mind was giving her an escape from where she was today, a pleasant thought to ease the tension and pain that she was actually feeling right at this moment.

The Submissive Scullery Maid
Shiralyn J. Lee

"Lidia, Lidia," Cassandra beckoned, "The vicar just asked you if you wanted to say a few words."

Lidia looked around at the crowd of mourners who were all waiting to hear her speak. "Yes, I'd like to say something. My husband was a good man, a great man and an extremely affectionate man. I will miss him tremendously—" A loud clap of thunder drowned out her voice and then a flash of lightening lit up the sky.

His coffin was laid to rest and Lidia was the first to throw a red carnation over the oak casket. It was his favourite flower and he often bought her a bouquet of them when he would return home from one of his supposed trips. Everyone had been soaked by the downpour, the grass had become sodden and Lidia's heels were sinking into it. Once the ceremony had been completed, she was accompanied by Cassandra back to the waiting carriage where the black horses wearing black plumes attached to their bridles, stood proud.

There was no conversation between the two women, it was better to be silent for now. The horses remained at walking pace—prolonging the journey. Lidia just closed her eyes and remembered snippets of happy thoughts with the man she had shared so much with. His face was already becoming hard for her to imagine, and in its place, images of Sally slowly filtered her mind. She was beginning to feel as though she was going crazy, and yelled out, "Why?"

The house was quiet, all staff remained silent and no chit chat went on. A few of Lidia's and her late husband's family and close friends came back to the house for the wake, mostly the older generation and snooty kind. Lidia could hardly wait for them to leave. She caught a glimpse of Sally as she handed out drinks and platters of sandwiches amongst the guests. Her beautiful red hair shone as she walked beneath the chandelier, and Lidia longed for her touch, she wanted to be with her—wanted desperately to make love with her.

"Lidia, I do hope that you'll still come and visit me, darling," her Aunt Emily suggested, as she stood blocking Lidia's view.

The Submissive Scullery Maid
Shiralyn J. Lee

"Yes, I will, I'll make sure that I do," she quietly replied trying to hide the longing in her teary eyes.

Sally was getting closer and Lidia hoped that they would be able to snare a moment. She caught another glimpse of a silver platter coming her way and as her aunt moved to the side, she now came face to face with Sally. A polite smile was exchanged between them. Sally's eyes were fixated on her lover as she offered her something from her platter. Lidia picked up a cucumber sandwich and a napkin. She couldn't eat but showed willing in front of her guests. It took a couple of hours until her last guest left, leaving her alone sitting in the red velvet high wing backed chair that she favoured. She could hear the sounds of the staff clearing up, so she got up and went to the door. Peering out into the hallway she saw Sally gathering up the remainders of sympathy cards and called her in to speak with her.

"How are you, Mrs. Cox, I mean considering the circumstances?" Sally asked politely.

"I'm fine, Sally, thank you for asking me. I just want you to know that I'm not ignoring you. In fact, it's been extremely hard seeing you and not being able to touch you, or kiss you. Even with my husband's death, I feel that I am losing my senses. I liked him very much but I love you."

Sally blushed. It was awkward for her to give herself under this roof. She wanted to tell Lidia that she would do anything for her but that conversation didn't take place. Instead, Lidia had some news of her own. She told Sally that she had given it a great deal of thought and that she had heard a short while ago that a small corner shop had been put up for sale. She'd purchased it before Mr. Cox's death and now had something on her hands that she had no use for. She made Sally an offer that was out of the blue.

"You can start your business as a dressmaker and I won't take no for an answer, Sally McGuire." Her insistence rang in Sally's ears as she tried to protest at such a generous offer.

91

The Submissive Scullery Maid
Shiralyn J. Lee

Sally didn't know what to say, the news had taken her by surprise. "But I don't understand, why would you...?"

"...Don't question, just accept my offer," she spoke softly, "You will be in possession of the keys this weekend." She turned to the sideboard and poured herself a brandy, looking into the mirror she could see a timid frightened girl standing behind her. All she wanted to do at this point was hold that beautiful girl in her arms but she knew that she had a duty as a widow to leave things as they are for now.

Sally couldn't believe what she was hearing, what was going to happen to her, what about her duties in the house, how was she going to pay for expenses. Everything she'd ever wanted had just been handed to her on a plate and yet she still felt empty. Was she being punished and sent away by the one person that she had grown to trust? Mrs. Cox began to explain everything, Sally would run the shop and choose what materials she needed, Lidia would fund it all, whatever Sally needed, she would get.

Three days later, a thrilled young-woman put the key in the lock and turned it. The small white wooden door with its tiny panes of glass, opened and Sally stepped into her own business. The shop was small but just big enough to cope with her needs. The front window bowed and Sally had an excellent view of both ends of the street.

She worked out a list of materials and silk threads and gave it to Lidia to take care of. Her shop was filled within the next few weeks and Sally was on her way to becoming a business woman. Lidia influenced her with the best clientele to seduce and once set up, Sally had already received three orders for dresses. Lidia slowly backed off from the decision making, leaving Sally fully in charge. With so much happening, Sally hadn't noticed that Lidia was drifting out of her life.

After a couple of months, Lidia informed her that she was going away for a while. She needed to console herself and become the

92

person she once was. Sally was saddened. This wasn't the way that things were supposed to work out between them. She had selfishly hoped that Lidia would come back to her, that they could secretly live their sordid life together under the eyes of unsuspecting friends.

The Submissive Scullery Maid
Shiralyn J. Lee

Chapter Ten

L idia had been gone for several weeks. Sally missed her like crazy but had to respect her wishes. She had to stay busy and think about making the business grow and get established, both for her and Lidia's sakes. She wore dresses that she'd made herself, in order to self-advertise as she paraded her wares down the high street and gained new customers.

Prostitutes were beginning to feel safe again, as there hadn't been any reported murders for a while and the police were focusing on several anonymous letters that they'd received.

A tall woman, elegantly dressed, walked into the shop. She snooped around for a while and huffed as she looked around at the high quality silks that Sally had on display.

"Oh, can I help you?" Sally asked as she emerged from the stock room.

"Yes. I was sent here by a friend. She recommended that I speak with you about an order I'd like to place."

"And what type of order would that be?" Sally asked as she plonked a roll of deep blue heavy satin into a corner.

"I'm under the impression that you are a very discreet girl."

"Yes, I am. Anything my clientele wishes to be confidential will stay that way."

The Submissive Scullery Maid
Shiralyn J. Lee

"Perfect, then I will proceed. Lidia mentioned that you may be interested in—"

"Lidia!" Sally cried out, "You've seen Lidia?"

"Why are you so startled by the mere mention of her name?" The woman paused. She stared into Sally's eyes. "You're the one, aren't you?" She asked inquisitively.

Sally stepped back, placing her hand on her chest. The mere mention of Lidia's name had taken her by surprise. The entrance door opened and another woman, apparently a friend to this customer, walked in. She was excited with some news that she'd just heard out in the street.

"They've just arrested the White Chapel Murderer. A small news boy just cried it out." Her eyes were wide and the smile on her face beaming as she sang it out to her friend.

The women all felt a moment of relief, every female in London had been feeling scared and nervous not knowing when this monster was going to strike again.

'So back to business," the tall woman requested. "I want you to make several of my ladies, some garments. I want them to be of an alluring nature. Corsets and knickers to be laced on the edges and deep sensuous colours are to be used. Can you do this?"

Sally nodded her head yes and the woman informed her that she would send her ladies in to be measured within the next couple of days. Sally was grateful for any kind of business, even if these ladies were providing sexual acts for pay.

Later that day a young woman with blonde curly hair and over done make up, came strolling in, humming a tune and acting in a fancy mood. Her one hand was rested on her hip and the other swinging a small purse around as if she was trying to make a spectacle of herself.

The Submissive Scullery Maid
Shiralyn J. Lee

"Good afternoon, Miss," she said to Sally as she carried on humming.

"Can I help you find something?"

"Well maybe you already have, I'm Lizzy, one of Angelique's girls. She came in earlier today about making us girls some sexy wot-nots." She brushed her curls back over her shoulders, revealing a rather pretty face, if she hadn't piled so much powder and colour on it.

"Oh, well I didn't expect anyone so soon, please come this way." She led Lizzy into the back where she could measure her in private. She wrote down the girl's size and showed her the different colours that she found suitable for her needs. Lizzy chose a deep plum with a black lace to trim it with. She saw herself as the head girl back at the parlour, so she felt that she should have the first choice and not be copied by the others. She was the competitive kind and wanted no one to be as good as she was in her profession.

"I've heard about you, you know." She had a smug look about her as if she had some kind of power over Sally.

"Oh, did Angelique mention my talent?"

"Nope. I heard about you from an old friend. She used to work at the parlour before meeting her rich husband. He was her Dark Cully and he fell in love with her, you know. Totally besotted with her, he was. She ain't ya typical dollymop, that one." Lizzy smiled but it wasn't a pleasant smile, more like, have I hurt you yet?

"Are you talking about Lidia?" Sally's heart jumped, Lidia had been hiding out just a few streets from her.

"Lidia, that's right, that's what she calls herself these days. She's at the parlour now, has been for a few weeks. I reckon she's trying to worm her way back in with Angelique but she won't have it, you know, and neither will I."

The Submissive Scullery Maid
Shiralyn J. Lee

Sally had to know more, she sat the girl down and offered her a cup of tea, the girl was impressed and felt like she was an important client. Sally questioned her about her lover, and found out that Lidia had run away from her family when she was sixteen. They had lined up a young gentleman to be her husband and she just couldn't allow herself to be touched by him. She'd kept in touch with her grandfather who has been extremely generous to her financially but she swore him to secrecy with her own parents. She had joined Angelique's parlour about seven years ago and became very popular with the local gentry. She was a toffer to them and that's how she earned her money. That's when John Cox fell in love with her. He would pay for her for the entire day, seven days a week. No other gent was allowed to touch her. He visited every day for a month until he whisked her away and married her. He knew that she came from money but she never had to worry about her finances once she married him.

"Please take me to the parlour, Lizzy." Sally's concern for her lover was genuine as she couldn't think of a worse place for her to be or even why she'd be there.

Lizzy was quite put out, she gave Sally a piece of her mind, being as she was a customer. Sally told her that she would make her corset extra special and that the other girls would be so jealous. Lizzy jumped at the chance and led Sally to the place where she worked.

It took twenty minutes to reach the parlour. Sally's heart was beating fast as Lizzy proudly showed off her new friend to the other girls as they walked in. Two girls sitting on a dark purple couch and wearing black lacy corsets and fishnet stockings, a look that any gentry would find appealing, stared at them as they approached. Lizzy told them to mind their own business if they knew what was good for them. She led Sally by her hand and traipsed her through the reception room with its dark furniture and heavy velvet drapes and into a back room, where sitting in a small red chair was Lidia. Sally's heart just melted as she laid her eyes on her lover once again.

"See. I told you she was here, but I ain't no blower," Lizzy insisted.

The Submissive Scullery Maid
Shiralyn J. Lee

"Lidia, what are you doing here?" Sally asked her as she sat at her feet and rested her head on her lap.

"Oh, my sweet girl," Lidia responded, looking down at the girl she loved and stroked her shiny red hair. Tears filled her eyes as her emotions took over. "I'm so sorry that I've hurt you. I should have kept you informed on what was going on but I didn't want you to be put in an awkward position."

"I don't understand, how could you put me in an awkward position, Lidia?"

"I'm being blackmailed. Cassandra demanded money from me to keep her mouth shut about my past. She was going to inform my father that I tip the velvet and that Jon was my Dark Cully. He would never be able show his face again, the shame he would feel." Her hands covered her face as she cried into them.

Sally felt powerless. All she could do now, was to get Lidia away from this bordello and safely back home, where they would have to figure out a way to rid Cassandra from their lives once and for all.

"Ere, you still gonna make my sexy wot-nots better than all the other gals. I ain't no snitch for free, you know," Lizzy piped up, her feet tapping as she waited impatiently for an answer.

"You'll get a good deal, Lizzy." Sally's tears began to match her lovers as they both left the house and made their way back to the shop through the back alleys, avoiding the local street market and bumping into anyone who knew Lidia by face.

They sat in the backroom of the shop and Sally made a fresh pot of tea. "Why did Cassandra turn on you like this, surely she would be putting her own reputation at risk as well as her marriage?"

"Her marriage is a farce. Her husband likes male company and that's why they are so well suited. She came to me and wanted to be treated like a whore, she wanted to be humiliated and fucked in front of you. I held the means but she held the power."

"Then she is living a life of lies herself and it should be her and her husband publicly humiliated." Sally was infuriated by this woman's demands and wondered just how she had the nerve to try and blackmail such a wonderful creature.

"I can't afford to get into a battle of rights, it's not just my reputation at risk, it's yours and John's and my family's good name. Business runs not just on the quality of production but also on a good family business name, if its reputation is tainted, it could be ruined in an instant."

Sally understood how Lidia had to protect everyone. She had a kind heart and only thought of others before her own needs. As they were talking, the shop door opened and a woman's voice called out. Sally went to see who it was and get rid of them. As she ventured out into the shop, she realised that it was Cassandra who had entered. She looked supreme in her deep blue silk dress and matching bonnet. Her jet black hair tied back with its perfect curls sitting exactly in place at the back. She was probably the most beautiful woman that Sally had ever laid her eyes on but her evilness was now showing through, making her look extremely unattractive.

"Hello, Sally, I see you've come up in the world." Her eyes beaded as she carefully gazed at her victim.

"What do you want, Cassandra?" Sally quickly snapped.

"So you must have spoken with Lidia by the tone of your voice. I told her not to have anything to do with you, if she knew what was good for her."

"You can't tell Lidia what to do, what right do you have, how could you be so callous?"

"I know she's here, I had you followed. Do you think Lizzy wouldn't squeal for the price of a drink?"

Lidia could hear the conversation taking place and came out into the shop front. She was angered by Cassandra's lack of respect toward Sally and begged Cassandra to quit whilst she still had the chance.

"Is that a threat to my good nature?" Cassandra asked her as she removed her velvet gloves and placed them inside her black velvet purse.

"Call it as you see it, all I see standing in front of me is a bitter woman with no morals," Lidia said firmly.

"There are so many things that I could tell you about your so called quaint little marriage. But one thing I would like to make clear, is that your so called loving husband was also rogering me. I told him about our little games on the day of his death." She gave a half smile from the corner of her mouth.

"You evil slut!" Sally slammed.

The three women began to raise their voices and no one could hear what the other was shouting. But the final argumentative words came from Cassandra as she yelled out above the other two, that John had gone to the Pig and Whistle to pick up a prostitute and have his wicked way with her. It was when they left the pub and stepped out into the street, drunken and fondling each other, that the black coach hit him whilst he was otherwise preoccupied. It was the prostitute's screaming and yelling for help that attracted the police to the scene and she was the one giving the idea that it was Jack the Ripper's coach.

Sally slapped her across her face and told her to never show her face again if she valued her life. Cassandra only smiled at the gesture, as if a mere scullery maid could threaten her well-being. She felt her cheek where she'd been struck and gestured to Sally that she might possibly one day be sorry for her actions. Sally wasn't the type of girl to feel threatened by such a tart and warned her to stay away, or she'd be the one to be sorry. Cassandra turned around and headed for the door but before leaving, she stated that she would be close by and expected her payment before the week was out. She told Lidia to meet her alone at the house on Friday evening and to have her cash ready, and then she exited the shop and disappeared down the high street and into the crowd of marketers.

Chapter Eleven

Friday evening had arrived and Lidia nervously waited for her nemesis to show her face. She drank a large glass of red wine to calm herself down as she sat anticipating Cassandra's demands. She drank another glass and then another and was now getting tipsy. By 9 o'clock Cassandra still hadn't arrived, causing Lidia to become agitated. At 9.30 p.m. a knock at the door startled Lidia and she heard Emily, her maid, answer to a female voice.

"I need to see Lidia immediately," Sally cried out.

Lidia immediately shot up out of her chair to greet her. Sally barged into the room and threw her arms around Lidia, pleased to see that she was all right. She was flush in her face and had been concerned about her lover's safety.

"So is she gone for good?" Sally asked as she scouted the room for any traces of a fight.

"She hasn't even shown her face, I have absolutely no idea where she might be."

They sat in front of the burning log fire waiting to be blackmailed by the wicked slut. Sally constantly looking to the street through the bay window to see if she could see the blackmailer. It was a long night and by 1 a.m. they were both asleep on the couch.

Morning arrived and they were awoken by Emily busily humming as she swept the hallway. Lidia's head was pounding as she stood up, causing her to sway. Sally was just plain exhausted from such a late night.

103

The Submissive Scullery Maid
Shiralyn J. Lee

They moved to the dining room for breakfast where the daily paper was waiting to be read on the table. Lidia picked it up as soon as she saw it. A picture of Cassandra was on the front page with the headline reading, 'MURDERED!' She gasped and fell into her seat. Sally ran to her aide and seeing the headline, went on to read just what had happened.

"Oh my god, she was murdered by her husband! He was arrested yesterday evening after fleeing from the murder scene. The maid had witnessed him strangle his wife in an attempt to silence her about his sexual preferences." Below in smaller writing an article read, 'Suspect released for the White Chapel Murders, police still hunting the Ripper.'

"Oh god, what if he knows about us, what if she told him everything?" Lidia shook her head, hoping that her namesake hadn't been compromised.

"I think that if she had, wouldn't the police have visited by now?"

"I'm not sure, Sally. The police sometimes take a while before responding to such allegations. We have to be on our guard."

"At least she won't be hounding us anymore!" Sally blurted out.

Three weeks went by and no one came to question either lady. Sally had managed to get her order fulfilled for Angelique's ladies, with Lizzie receiving the best looking corset. In the meantime, she had made a couple of garments for private use for her and Lidia. They focused on going to the country house this coming weekend and sex was on the menu.

Sally packed a bag containing the items that she had designed solely for their game play. She looked forward to finally being with Lidia sexually. Lidia had hinted that she wanted to be in control and act as Sally's mistress. Sally had liked what she had seen in this behavior

104

and so accepted Lidia's wish. Upon entering the country house, Lidia immediately went into her role as mistress and commanded Sally to go to her bedroom and strip naked. She was to wait for her by the bed. In the meantime Lidia changed into her garments that her lover had provided. A corset made from the finest silk in a rich red and black trims running vertically over the whalebone structure. Her breasts were pushed up high and bursting over the top with diamantes edging the bust line and a black lace frill to edge the bottom. The back had just a small area to lace the corset together and then below she had adorned a black ruffle just covering Lidia's buttocks. Velvet bows had been attached to the tops of her stockings and she wore a matching velvet chocker that fitted snug around her neck. She let her long hair down and ruffled it slightly to give herself an alluring look.

Sally waited naked and patiently by the end bedpost, she was sexually aroused and needed to be fucked. She could hear Lidia as she climbed the stairs and closed her eyes, waiting for her mistress to command her to look at her. Lidia entered the room, her first instruction was for Sally to open her eyes and look at the woman who was going to fuck her. Sally was impressed when she caught sight of Lidia's beauty—she had made the perfect outfit for the occasion.

"Put your hands behind you!"

Lidia took hold of Sally's hands behind her back and placed a leather strap around her wrists, tying her to the bed post. She kicked Sally's legs apart, tying one ankle to the post that she was held by and then a longer length of leather attaching her other ankle to the post on the other end of the bed. Sally was spread wide and excited for the next move. Lidia put a blindfold around her eyes and then set to work. Kneeling down in front of Sally, she began to blow gently into her pink folds. Sally twitched as she felt the nice sensation. Then Lidia pushed a cucumber into Sally's vagina. Sally groaned as she received the object without knowing what had entered her. Lidia slid it up and down, fucking her lover as she pleased. Sally bit her lower lip, trying to take the pain, her body confused by liking such torture.

The Submissive Scullery Maid
Shiralyn J. Lee

"Take it, you fucking whore," she taunted her captive.

Sally liked to hear Lidia call her sluttish names, it turned her on even more and now she was enjoying her sex toy, Lidia removed it from her and threw it on the ground. She moved in close and began to lick Sally's organ, just using the tip of her tongue to tease her pearl. Sally's legs began to quiver, she wanted to lie on her back and take her pleasure but she had to take it as her mistress wished her to. Lidia decided to take it to a different level and untied her girl, taking her to the punishment room. She tied her wrists to a chain that hung from the ceiling. Sally was powerless and her submissiveness pleased her mistress. Lidia teased her by tickling her face with a feather; Sally kept pulling her face away from it, as the tease irritated her. Lidia then stroked the feather down her neck and over her breasts. She tickled her stomach and then her inner thighs. Sally wriggled, she liked it but not knowing what was touching her, made her giggle and Lidia slapped her backside to control her.

With her arms trussed up, Lidia decided to give her a punishment fit for her insubordination. She picked up two bamboo brushes and began to lash Sally's buttocks. Her cheeks were reddening and beginning to sting but still, Lidia lashed her girl. Sally tried to clench her cheeks as she received the whips, so Lidia reminded her about the ginger root. Sally had to relax. She knew the sensation that the ginger would give, so she began to behave herself. Lidia stopped the lashing and released her lover from her restraint. Laying her on her back on the wooden floor, she crouched between her thighs and seduced her subject by kissing her inner thighs and stomach, teasing and exciting her to make her needs intense. Sally opened her legs wide, she had to be fucked— to be licked. She needed to accomplish an orgasm. Lidia positioned her tongue and gave long slow strokes over her clit. Sally's body twitched and her breathing became concentrated as she felt her insides changing. Lidia licked hard and fast, as Sally arched her back, enjoying the service that she was receiving.

The Submissive Scullery Maid
Shiralyn J. Lee

Lidia licked and licked, until Sally lost control over her body and came into the mouth that teased her. They laid on the floor, interlinking their legs and arms, Sally exhausted and well-spent and Lidia proud that she'd accomplished her goal.

This was a house that they felt safe in, a house where no one could possibly interfere with their lifestyle. Lidia's mind began to work hard, her thoughts trailing into a life with Sally. She had the idea that the two of them should live in this house, keep their lives secret and away from the intrusion of prying eyes and gossiping wenches.

Sally entertained the idea of the two of them living together as a couple, she knew it would be dangerous, as in the eyes of the law, this wasn't possible but her love for Lidia had a power so intense that nothing else mattered.

It was from this moment on that on week days, they spent in the City, living a life of lies but caring for business and occasionally Sally would visit Eveleen and Abigail, and on the weekends they spent their valuable time at the country house, living out their fantasies with Sally being a submissive and Lidia her mistress.

The Submissive Scullery Maid
Shiralyn J. Lee

Chapter Twelve

Lidia's Story
Love for Lidia

On her 13th birthday, Lidia was introduced to Thomas Thorpe, the son of Charles Thorpe, owner of several factories and mills in the area. For the next three years she was encouraged to keep in good company with Thomas. Her father had betrothed his daughter to this boy and when she was old enough they would marry. It wasn't even due to the fact that they needed a good dowry to survive under the Victorian rule but more so that their daughter would be guaranteed a wealthy future. Her happiness had been overlooked by all involved, even by Mr. Charles Thorpe himself.

Thomas was the kind of lad who showed signs of cruelty. He had a way about him, as if everything and everyone he came across, he just happened to take an instant dislike to. On one occasion he had mentioned to Lidia that he wanted to give one of the workers at his father's factory a lesson that he would remember for the rest of his life. All this worker had done was to show his superior that they had made a mistake in the order that they were taking care of. Thomas saw it as insubordination and if it were up to him, he would have sent this man on his way in an instant.

On Lidia's 16th birthday, her father gave a party for her, inviting everyone of importance, just for show. He bought her a dress fit for a princess, a pink ball gown with a delicate lace trim. She had a look of innocence about her.

It was during this party that Thomas held his stemmed glass in the air and tapped on it with a small silver knife. Everyone turned to see what he was doing. He told everyone that he had an announcement to make, one that would be pleasing to their ears. He announced that he and Lidia were now engaged! Lidia was horrified. She had no idea that this was going to happen. Her heart pounded hard in her chest, her mind raced and her stomach turned in disgust. She had unwittingly been set up by the one person she thought that she could trust—her father!

As the guests all held their glasses up to make a toast to the good news, Lidia stepped back towards the open door behind her. It led out onto the patio and then a large lawn area surrounded it. She found herself not just walking but actually racing down the driveway. She was breathless and scared. As she was running so fast she got the stitch and had to crouch down near a small brook, hiding from sight of anyone who dared look for her.

She waited, tucked into a ditch just by the edge of the road until the evening sky appeared. Luckily it was warm, and as she traipsed across the fields to avoid being found, she caught the bottom of her dress, ripping its beautiful trim. Tears filled her eyes as she began to wonder why she was even in this predicament. How could her father have sneaked behind her back and done this to her. She stopped dead in her tracks and fell to the ground. Slumped in the middle of a field of red poppies, she broke down and let her emotions take control. Her cheeks were stained with her tears and her dress stained with green marks from the grass that lay beneath her. She ended up sleeping in that field until the pink dawn sky and the chirping birds disturbed her rest.

She found herself walking through several fields, down long narrow lanes, avoiding any contact with any other person who may report seeing her. Coming across a small cottage, she waited behind a bush, watching to see if anyone was home. After hiding for what seemed like hours but was probably only a few minutes, she noticed a large woman coming out of the back door. She was holding a large wicker basket filled with wet washing. Pegging it out on a rope that had been erected from the side wall of the house to a tall tree at the end of the garden, she caught sight of Lidia crouching behind her Rhododendron bush.

"Hello, Miss, can I help you?" she asked as she walked over to the wooden fence that surrounded her small piece of land.

"Um, no. I was just, just on my way," Lidia stammered. She was scared that she was going to be frog marched right back to her house.

"I haven't seen you around these parts before, where are you from?"

"I'm...I'm..." Tears flowed down her cheeks as she had no answer to give this woman.

The woman approached her and bent down. Studying her face she calmly said, "Come on inside the house, my dear child, let me make you a nice cup of tea and we can talk about anything you care to."

Lidia dried her eyes on the frill that trimmed the neckline of her dress. She followed the kind lady into her house and sat on an oak wooden chair at the kitchen table. The woman introduced herself as Margaret, and gave Lidia a warm currant scone that she had just baked and a hot cup of tea. She told her that she would feel much better after this little tid-bit. Lidia scoffed her cake quickly, she hadn't eaten since yesterday morning and had been feeling rather dizzy the last couple of hours. She was thankful for this woman's kindness.

"Come, my dear, help me hang these sheets out on the washing line and then we can make a start on supper. I can see that even a little might like you needs to eat a proper meal."

"Yes, thank you, I'd be very happy to help you." Lidia smiled at her and jumped off the chair ready to take on her task.

She had no idea how to hang out sheets or any other type of laundry. Margaret laughed as she watched Lidia struggle. She helped her out but carried on laughing at the sight that she had been given.

111

The Submissive Scullery Maid
Shiralyn J. Lee

"My name is Lidia," she said as she joined in the laughter.

"Well child, with a name like that, I can see why you don't know how to hang out sheets."

After the washing had been hung, Margaret gave Lidia a nice cold glass of milk and they sat on a small wooden bench by the back door just watching the bumble bees fly by and collect their nectar and listened to the sounds of the singing birds.

They sat for a while until Margaret suggested that they better get the supper started. She put logs inside the burner and lit the huge oven. Whilst that warmed up, she showed Lidia how to prepare a chicken. It had been hanging upside down in her shed for two days and was ready for the next process. She chopped its neck off and feet and washed the bird in a bucket of water. Placing it in a pan ready for the oven, she basted it with lard. She hummed as she laid some sprigs of rosemary and stuffed a whole lemon inside its cavity.

Lidia felt at home with this woman and in the short few hours that she'd known her, she realised that it was the most relaxed that she'd ever felt in her life.

"I ran away and I'm not going back," she blurted out to her new friend.

"So what are you running from, my sweet child?"

"My future!"

"Well now, how can that be, how can you run from what hasn't happened yet?"

"It was just about to. My father has planned to marry me off to someone so awful. I didn't even know that he had already set it all up until yesterday." Her chin began to quiver as she thought about her father's callousness.

The Submissive Scullery Maid
Shiralyn J. Lee

"Well, you're safe here tonight, I can't say for sure how my husband will feel about you being here but I'm sure that he wouldn't turn away such a pretty little thing like you."

It was now 7 p.m. The bird was cooked and the roast potatoes were just being plated. Margaret had cooked long green beans and carrots that she'd grown herself in her garden. It was now 7.10 p.m. and her husband was walking up the pathway toward the house. He removed his boots at the front door and kicked them to the side, his shirt was filthy and his trousers covered in dry mud.

"Hello, my dear, did you have a hard day at work?"

"I bloody fell over this morning on my way. That bloody dog down the lane chased me again and I ran straight into a ditch." He tugged at his trouser legs to show his wife how filthy he actually was.

"Oh never mind, soon you can have a wash and I'll get those clothes nice and fresh for you for the morning. We have a guest, her name is Lidia, says she ran away from her future."

"Oh did she now? How can she be doing that when it hasn't happened yet?"

Lidia and Margaret giggled as he'd repeated almost word for word the comment made earlier. They sat around the table and Margaret and her husband Bill, held hands ready to say grace. Margaret offered Lidia her other hand to take and all three of them closed their eyes as Bill said a few grateful words followed by Amen.

"This smells so good, Margaret. I never knew that cooking could be such a delight."

"Delight, what kind of talk is this?" Bill quizzed as he pulled a leg off the bird and planted it on his plate.

The Submissive Scullery Maid
Shiralyn J. Lee

"I think she means that she enjoyed working in the kitchen with me. Hasn't had much opportunity by the looks of things," Margaret informed her husband.

Lidia ate everything on her plate and even had seconds. Her hosts looked amazed as they couldn't believe how much she'd eaten for such a small creature. But Lidia had already set her mind on the next day's travels. She would eat big tonight because she had no idea where her next meal was coming from.

Margaret offered her a bed for the night and she gratefully accepted the kind offer. The bed mattress was a little lumpy, Lidia was used to her home comforts and apart from last night's field of poppies, this was the first time in her life that she had slept on anything other than her own bed. The sheets were crisp and clean and smelt fresh and with the window open, allowing a warm summer breeze to flow into the room, she soon fell asleep. Margaret checked in on her before she too retired for the night, she smiled when she saw a troubled girl have a peaceful look on her face as she slept.

The sun shone through the window, casting its beams across the room. Tiny dust particles danced around as the rays caught them in its path. Lidia woke, stretching her arms wide and yawning loudly. She felt relaxed and ready to conquer whatever the day wanted to throw at her.

Entering the kitchen, she found Margaret busy cooking a breakfast of bacon and fried eggs.

"Sit down my child, let me feed that big appetite of yours. Bill has left for the day but he did say that it was nice to meet you." She plonked three strips of bacon and two eggs on a blue willow patterned plate.

Lidia was impressed by her china. She'd got her best out just for her guest. Lidia ate it all up and then informed Margaret that she had no way to repay her kindness. Margaret didn't mind, she liked having the girl around. It had made a pleasant change to her routine days. Lidia informed her that she had to leave as she was planning on making her way to London. She had made her mind up and was determined to get there before nightfall. Margaret told her that she knew someone who could take her into the City. He would be calling by shortly to see if she needed anything picking up. She would ask Tim if he wouldn't mind a little company on his way in to the City. After Lidia had finished her food, she washed up her plate and cutlery and thanked Margaret for being such a wonderful person. She told her that she would always remember her in her prayers.

Margaret gave Lidia a package containing pieces of chicken, raw carrots and a large slice of apple pie. She also gave her a few shillings, something that she had been saving for a rainy day but she felt that Lidia had a greater need for it than she did. She told her that at least it would be enough to give her a couple of night's board and keep her safely off the streets and away from evil doers.

The Submissive Scullery Maid
Shiralyn J. Lee

Chapter Thirteen

L idia's arm ached as she frantically waved goodbye to her new friend as she and Tim set off towards London. Two black horses pulled their cart and Tim had them trotting along the dirt track until they reached the lane that headed in the direction of the City. He slowed the horses down and began to whistle a tune that he liked. Lidia sat quietly next to him. It was a little awkward at first, he being a shy boy and she being a beautiful girl. She could see from the corner of her eye that he kept sneaking in a peek of her, every now and again.

"So where are you headed to?" he finally managed to ask.

"I'm not really sure, my Grandfather lives there so maybe if I can get him to keep my whereabouts a secret, I will stay under his roof."

"Well maybe I should take you directly to him, you know, make sure that you're safe, an' all." He carried on whistling his tune and he had a smile about him as if he was pleased with himself. "So are you walking out with anyone in particular, I don't mean to be intrusive but you're a pretty girl and I think you'll soon be taken by a man if you're not."

"I was, but I'm not interested anymore. Right now I have to concentrate on getting my life in order."

It took two and half hours until they reached the outskirts of London. Lidia began to feel sad, she was missing her father, and even if he had pre-arranged her future, she still had a bond with him. A tear escaped from the corner of her eye and she discreetly wiped it away before

The Submissive Scullery Maid
Shiralyn J. Lee

Tim saw that she was getting emotional. They headed toward Islington, where her Grandfather had a small property, one of many that he owned in the City but this is the one that he chose to reside in.

It was almost midday when they reached his house. Tim helped her down from the cart and waited whilst she knocked on the door. A woman dressed in a plain black dress and looking rather irritated that she'd been called to answer the door, waited for Lidia to announce why she was standing on the doorstep.

"Hello, I'm Lidia, Lidia Wainwright. I believe that My Grandfather lives here." She looked at the woman with angst. She dreaded being turned away by her.

"Lidia, little Lidia?" she said as she came to realisation that Lidia wasn't so little anymore.

"Is my Grandfather here, could I possibly see him?" Lidia asked as she tried to sneak a look past the woman's shoulder and inside the hallway.

"Why yes he is, come in my child, come in." She clasped her hands over her mouth and stepped aside to let the girl in.

Lidia looked back at Tim and gave him a small wave to let him know that she was okay. He smiled back and then left to carry out his own errands. The woman led Lidia through the dark hallway and up a small flight of stairs to a room where her Grandfather was seated by the window.

"I think you have a visitor, Mr. Wainwright," she announced to him.

He turned around and right away he recognised his visitor. His smile was beaming as he got up to greet her and welcome her into his home. Lidia explained to him everything that had been going on with her arranged marriage and how distraught she was. He sympathised with her needs and understood why she had chosen to run away. He hated her father, even though he was his own flesh and blood. They hadn't spoken in years and her Grandfather was certain that he would never talk to his son again. He made a promise to Lidia that her whereabouts would never be discovered from his lips. Her secret was his secret. Lidia felt at peace and made herself comfortable over the next couple of days. Her Grandfather enjoyed having her around, she gave him life again, made him realise that he had a purpose in life.

On the third day of her visit her Grandfather received a telegram. It was from her own father, he had sent out a request that if she was to turn up in his company that he was to immediately have her escorted home. He tore the paper up and threw it into the fire and watched it burn.

"You need a place where you can be safe. Somewhere that no one would find you." He thought for a while, with his hand brushing the bottom of his chin he suddenly came up with a solution. "I have a house that I've kept secret from everyone. It's my safe place where I can escape the annoying City and its diseases of cholera and the starving homeless."

He had his housekeeper measure Lidia up for a selection of new silk dresses and to have them sent to the house in Harrow. Then he had her order them a carriage to take them straight to Harrow. The house itself was huge and at first Lidia felt intimidated by its grandeur but she soon fitted in.

This is where she called home for the next two years. She'd grown to love the house, her Grandfather left her alone in fear that he could possibly be followed by someone her father would have hired, so he just sent the occasional letter to make sure everything was in order and that Lidia was safe. But as Lidia was entering womanhood and beginning to feel unsettled through lack of a social life, she'd been thinking about venturing back to Islington, now that her father's search had died off. She would find herself a friend of some sort, a companion, someone whom she could share her thoughts with.

The Submissive Scullery Maid
Shiralyn J. Lee

She made it her mission to venture deep into the City and found herself sitting in the middle of the park just watching the world pass by. She must have been there for about an hour when a woman, with a head full of red hair, dressed in pale pink attire and beige gloves, sat beside her. She sat silently for a few minutes, her eyes watching, just as Lidia's were.

"The birds are so free, aren't they?" she said softly.

"I suppose so," Lidia replied.

"Please forgive my rudeness. I'm Angelique. I like to come here and escape the reality."

"I see what you mean." Lidia agreed. "I'm Lidia."

They shook hands and began to chat politely. Lidia found Angelique to be rather intriguing and mysterious. She had a way of answering questions indirectly, leaving Lidia none the wiser. After spending a couple of hours chatting away, they decided to meet up on a regular basis. The park would be their meeting point and they would be able to exchange pleasantries between themselves. Lidia had a good feeling about this woman and was happy that she'd instantly found a friend.

As the weeks went on, the two women found themselves meeting up more frequently. They had an attraction towards each other, it was stronger than just a friendship and Lidia felt her insides tingle each time they met up. She wanted to be in Angelique's presence as often a she could without understanding why.

It was when their relationship had formed into a close friendship, that Angelique asked Lidia if she'd be interested in visiting her place of work. Lidia was excited to go, so that afternoon they headed off back to Angelique's mysterious business premises.

A short way into the city and down a small narrow alley way, Angelique introduced Lidia to a building with not much to show for itself. The plain red brick wall and a black door fitted with brass accessories, weren't much to look at. But once inside, Lidia found herself daunted by the image that she had been presented with. Red feather boas draped around the shelves that held the brass lamps and dark wooded walls complimented with oil paintings with scantily clad women. But the most shocking sight to her eyes was the fact that a group of women, all of them barely wearing anything, were sitting around on velvet sofas and high winged back chairs. One girl was smoking a long cigar and another was fixing her stockings to fit perfectly around the top of her thighs.

"Bought us another gal, I see," one of them piped up.

"Blimey, she better had put a smile on her face, she's too serious looking for the likes of this place."

"Cut it out, ladies. This is my new friend Lidia. Say hello to her."

The women reluctantly greeted her, they saw her as a new competitor in their business but Lidia was unaware of what kind of business they were in to. One of the women sat with her one leg dangling over the arm of the couch, she wore stockings edged with red silk garters and a black lace corset that had been tailored so that she could remove it in a quick moment of passionate fondling.

Angelique led her through the lounge and into a back room where they would have more privacy. Lidia sat in a chair and Angelique poured her a glass of red wine. She explained to Lidia that she was in an industry that most upstanding citizens would certainly disapprove of. The look on Lidia's face showed her new friend that she was completely innocent when it came to sexual practice and any knowledge connected to the secret sex act.

"I used to be a prostitute on the street but then a kind gentleman left me his entire fortune when he passed away. This is what I did with my inheritance and I'm quite proud of it. The girls are safe and get treated accordingly by my guests and I feel that with the added bonus of privacy, my clientele are able to receive the service that they so desire."

"May I ask what service that you are referring to?" Lidia asked sweetly.

Angelique laughed. She was in the presence of a virgin. This was something that didn't happen too much in her line of work. "My girls give a service to gentlemen of a higher class. We entertain judges, high ranking police officers and many more. I'm always on the lookout for a new girl to capture the eyes of my paying customers, if you were ever interested, I know you'd fetch a pretty penny."

Lidia almost choked on her drink. Never once had she entertained the idea of giving herself to a total stranger and for money too. She had been appalled by the mere thought that she almost had to be touched by the hands of Thomas Thorpe. This would certainly be an outrageous idea.

Angelique, realising that she had insulted her new friend began to apologise immediately, it had always been in her nature to be so upfront and personal with the girls that she happened to come across in her life.

"So I see that it's getting dark outside, rather than travelling back at this hour on your own, why don't you stay for the evening? I'm sure I could entertain you somehow." As she sat down in the chair opposite Lidia, she adjusted her bodice and swept her hair back behind her shoulders. Her cheek bones were perfect, her eyes sparkled and her lips looked tasteful.

Lidia felt a stir inside her stomach, unsure of why, she kept staring Angelique's face. Her mouth turned dry, her mind began to race and her chest felt tight. She couldn't breathe. Angelique noticed that something was wrong and was at her side in an instant.

"My poor girl, are you all right?"

The Submissive Scullery Maid
Shiralyn J. Lee

"I...I...I feel sick!" She gasped for her next breath and Angelique undid the buttons on the back of her dress to allow her to breathe properly.

"Okay, let me fetch you a glass of water." Angelique poured her a drink and enticed her to sip on it slowly. Patting her forehead with a cool damp cloth, she started to hum a tune in aid to soothe Lidia's condition.

Lidia liked the way that she touched her so gently. She possessed a power over Lidia's mind, a kind of physical force that she wanted more of. As Angelique knelt in front of her, looking up into her confusion, she leant down and stole a kiss from her lips. Angelique didn't shy away from her unexpected advance. In fact, she repaid the kiss with one of her own. For the first time in her life, Lidia felt comfortable with her actions. It was a passionate kiss. One that made Lidia's inside's tingle with excitement.

"You surprised me, Lidia, I'm sure that I would never have guessed that you felt this way about me."

"I didn't even know myself until now," Lidia exclaimed.

"Come with me." Angelique led her out of the room and into another down the hallway. It was a bedroom with a four poster bed draped with dark red velvet curtains and edged with gold tassels. Deep burgundy walls and a dark oak wood floor gave it a sultry image, one that would seduce even the shyest of people.

Lidia began to tremble, she had never given herself to anyone, but Angelique knew that she was still a virgin, so she sat her on the edge of the bed. Looking deeply into Lidia's eyes she gently brushed the back of her hand over her cheek and glided her finger over her lower lip. Lidia responded by giving her finger a light bite as a tease to take things further. She began to breathe hard and fast, the hairs on her arms standing on edge and her thoughts sending crazy messages inside her body. Angelique began to undress. She removed her gown easily, revealing a deep blue silk corset with ruffles on the lower back and lace trim around the top. She turned around and asked Lidia to undo the laces. Lidia hesitated for a moment, admiring the structure of Angelique's body, she found herself loosening the laces and prizing the corset open. Angelique stepped out of it and turned back around to face Lidia.

"Now let me undress you," she whispered as she took Lidia by her hand and encouraged her to stand before her.

She kissed Lidia's neck and exposed chest area. Her hands held on gently to her waist as she tormented her lover's skin with her seduction. Lidia closed her eyes and longed for more of this. Angelique moved behind her and unbuttoned her dress. A tall mirror propped up against the wall gave Angelique the opportunity to see Lidia's reaction as she swept it open, she revealed Lidia's upper back, the white silky skin tone had never been seen by anyone else and Lidia began to feel a sexual sensation. She allowed her dress to fall to the ground. Her corset, white and lacy, was the next garment for Angelique to remove. She kissed Lidia's shoulder as she unlaced the strings and pushing the corset down and over Lidia's thighs, she clasped her hands over her breasts, caressing the mounds. Lidia placed her hands over them and as Angelique slid her hands down her flat stomach and over her hip bones, she became sexually aroused. She watched herself in the mirror being seduced by such a beautiful woman. Angelique coaxed her on to the bed and kissed her from her mouth down her neck over her breasts and her ribcage. She reached her stomach and began to lick in circular motions. Lidia was excited and Angelique could smell her sexual juices as she proceeded further down. She prized her legs open—her breath could be felt as she blew gently over Lidia's clit.

"I'm going to taste you now. You're never going to feel the same again," she stated as she moved in closer to Lidia's organ.

Lidia arched her back as Angelique's warm wet tongue licked over her clit. She whimpered with joy as she felt it again and again and her

124

stomach flipped with a feeling of excitement. She gripped the sheets tightly as her legs trembled and twitched. Her loss of control over her body excited her and she wanted to scream out. She had no idea that this was how it was going to feel and she wanted it, she wanted it to last forever. Angelique began to lick faster and the tip of her tongue teased Lidia's clit. Her blood was flowing faster now and her sweat had built up, her clit had become engorged and her mind receiving so many mixed confused messages. The sensations inside her were changing and she could feel something else happening, her body began to jolt and her eyes rolled back. Her vagina began to spasm and a sudden explosive sensation erupted from her insides. Lidia had just experienced her first sexual act—she was now in a euphoric state of mind.

The next few months were life changing for Lidia. She had transformed her lifestyle, her relationship with Angelique had blossomed and she was deeply in love. She'd even been privy to watch how the ladies performed their sexual acts on their rich clients. She became intrigued by how the girls had total control over these men and women, how they were able to torture and humiliate them in front of onlookers and yet not be disparaged by it all. One client, a judge, actually asked for Lidia to perform his next beating. Angelique had been giving her lessons in how to be the aggressor, the Mistress, the one who holds the authority. Lidia had been a good student. She learned quickly and had given a few clients a small taste of what she was about.

Her interest in men sexually was none existent but she knew that there was a lot of money to be made out of this business, so she compromised by dishing out their requests but never allowed them to touch her. She was a tease. Nearly every client had by now, requested her at some point, as news of her virginity to men was spreading. Each one of them thinking that they would be the one to break her in, but Angelique had been the one to do that task already.

The Submissive Scullery Maid
Shiralyn J. Lee

Lidia's first client, the judge, a big fat man balding and sweaty, was laid on his front. His big hairy fat arse was her target. She had in her hands a pair of brush floggers, striking his fat buttocks, she tormented him verbally.

"How much do you think I'm worth, you greedy man," she taunted, "You deserve no better than a dog."

He begged her for forgiveness, he wanted her to beat him but he also wanted to act like a snivelling idiot, something so diverse from his normal life. As a judge, he was a cruel man, he acted like a god, treated people like scum and gained excessive amounts of money in bribing and controlling the weak and unfortunate people who came across his wrath. He knew that his acts were wrong so in his twisted mind he considered being beaten by a beautiful woman was justification in itself. Lidia in her wisdom used this to her advantage. She would occasionally whip him a little harder in his sensitive parts and then tell him that that strike was worth double the amount of money that he was paying and he being so grateful, paid it.

She got him to stand up and walk over to the wall, his stomach, covered in stretch marks, hung over the tops of his thighs but all she saw was coin in her purse. Chains that had been attached to the bricks dangled down, leather straps were attached to the ends. With his wrists in restraints, she was able to flog his thighs and legs as well and with a little gentle persuasion she was also able to get him to beg her for mercy and that he was to pay her extra if she went easier on him. She would flog him even harder than he deserved, so that when she eased up on it, he would feel that she was being kinder and would actually be gratified over the process.

This was only the beginning of her underground career. She had the best reputation any girl in this business had. After two years of building her clientele up, she began to receive the attention of a certain young woman. At least once a week she'd make an appointment for Lidia to service her. Angelique would sometimes join in as an added affect to the game and she worked well with Lidia. Their romantic

126

relationship had diminished over the last few months but their friendship remained as strong as ever. Lidia knew what she was about and where her life was headed, she was in to women only, whereas Angelique liked to fool around with the gentlemen that she'd become acquainted with. This wasn't for Lidia, she had bigger plans with her life, she was just waiting for the right person to come along, someone who could share her passion and her secrets.

Her female client, Cassandra, would opt for Lidia to humiliate her in front of others. She had no morals. Her audience would be made up of the ladies of the house and a few male clients who were being serviced at the time of her appointment. Only Lidia was allowed to touch her body. Cassandra's beauty was outstanding, her long black curly hair and her full red lips were enough to make any woman lust after her and any man want to see her punished and humiliated in order to get their own satisfaction. Lidia was more than happy to touch her skin, she was soft and silky, and her eyes were dark and lustful and drew Lidia instantly.

She had her parading around naked on all fours whilst clientele entered the parlour; Cassandra loved it and couldn't get enough of Lidia's control. She was married to a man much older than herself and as for sex with him, he was past doing anything in the bedroom years ago.

Lidia made her crawl to the back bedroom, her backside on show and her vagina exposed, she entered the room and Lidia slammed the door shut behind her. She made her lie down on the bed, her arms stretched out to the sides of the bed and her legs opened wide. Lidia strapped her ankles to the posts at the bottom of the bed and her wrists to the top posts. She placed a blindfold over her eyes and told her to be quiet.

Cassandra was a slut, she liked to be fucked, she liked it hard and she wanted it right now. Lidia tormented her. She touched between her legs, slowly gliding her fingers towards Cassandra's wet opening. She quickly pulled her fingers away just as Cassandra thought she was going to enter her. Lidia had a cucumber and touched Cassandra's opening with the tip of it, its coldness intrigued Cassandra, her mind now wondering what it was. Lidia pushed it inside her a little and then began to fuck her subject slowly. Cassandra enjoyed this, she wanted more, she wanted the pain and the pleasure.

"Fuck me," she cried out, as she squirmed and jolted.

"I told you to be quiet, slut!" Lidia snapped. She rammed the cucumber in harder, Cassandra whimpered.

Satisfied with hurting her client, she left the cucumber inside her and with a flogging brush in each hand, she began to flog Cassandra's body from her chest, over her belly and down each leg. Red thrash marks began to appear over her skin but it didn't deter her subject from wanting more. Lidia untied her and removed the long vegetable and then commanded her to turn over and rest on her hands and knees. With her buttocks facing Lidia and her face buried into the sheets, she received her next round of punishment. Lidia thrashed her cheeks, the harder the better for Cassandra, each stroke that brushed her skin stung more than the last one but there were no words of stop, no actions of forced cruelty and no signs of passion.

Cassandra rocked her body, she welcomed her punishment. Lidia gave her one last whip with the brushes before stroking her buttocks gently with her hands to keep them from stinging too much.

"No one hurts me like you do, Lidia," Cassandra commended her.

Lidia smiled, knowing how Cassandra liked to be treated like a common slut. She handed her a robe to put on and as Cassandra got up she found it hard to walk. Her cheeks were sore but she liked that feeling, and with Lidia's assistance, she dressed and left, heading off to go and live the sad boring life that her aging husband offered her.

As Lidia became well sought after in her role as a Mistress, she gained a new client, John Cox. He was a man who held a high status in his circle of friends and keeping his private life extremely private he became besotted with Lidia. It didn't take long before he was paying for her time on a daily basis. His wealth showed as he requested that she would no longer entertain any other clients and he would provide her with enough money to cover her loss of expenses. Lidia admired his arrogance, it became a turn on for her and she soon became fond of him. He quickly fell in love with her and asked for her hand in marriage. Even though she was completely in to women, it didn't take her long to decide to accept his offer and within weeks of meeting him they were soon married. She never proclaimed her undying love for him, after all, he was a man but she needed security in her life and under the rule of Queen Victoria there was no such thing as lesbianism. John had the attitude that if he had enough love for them both that their marriage would be one of a strong bond. But Lidia had settled, she was at the point in her life where she was growing restless and if Jon was paying for her continually, then she might as well just marry the man.

They had a quiet wedding, just a handful of friends and John's parents. Lidia was accepted by John's crowd, her beauty and her polite personality had won them over. She had a few acquaintances of her own, Cassandra had remained a social friend and one older lady that Lidia called Aunt Emily, John would never be the wiser to any acts that had taken place with these women and as far as Aunt Emily, well she really was like an aunt.

During the next four years, Lidia lived a life of lies, her inner soul was crying out, desperate for attention from the female kind. John was a good man to her, he knew that things weren't right but he overlooked that matter. As time went on, Lidia grew unsettled and any acts of intimacy between her and her husband became few and far between. John began to seek out prostitutes once again, he thought that he was being discreet but Lidia knew exactly what he was up to. They managed to somehow not let this matter bother them as Lidia had found her outlet too. She and Cassandra would spend opportune days at her country house that her grandfather had leased her. She had kept this house a secret from John, it was her escape and the fact that she'd had one of the bedrooms fitted with ropes and chains and used it as a torture room, wouldn't have gone down too well with him.

It was Friday morning and breakfast was being served. John had his face buried in the newspaper as Lidia walked into the room. She admired the fragrant white roses that had been arranged in a tall glass vase and sat proudly in the centre of the table and took note to remember to tell Lilly that she had done a wonderful job polishing the silver candelabras.

"There's been a murder in White Chapel," he proclaimed to his wife as he began to fold the paper.

"In White Chapel, does it say who?" Lidia quickly asked as she knew many women from that area.

"No one to worry about, it looks like she was a common prostitute. The police aren't too concerned by what I can tell." He placed the paper down on the table and didn't give the story a second thought.

Lidia felt for the community, she knew that something like this would have the women scared out of their wits. Thank god Angelique had had the sense to invest in her own private building.

"So I've hired a new scullery maid, she seems like a sweet natured girl and she's got a slight Irish accent." John giggled as he informed his wife about their new employee.

"Well that's wonderful." Lidia's reply was nonchalant as her concern was with the women of the street. She sipped on her morning tea and only took one bite from her toast as her appetite had left her.

Her husband finished his breakfast and left to go to his morning meeting. Lidia sat for a while and stared out of the window, watching the rain drops trickle down the pane of glass. Her mood was sad and she found it hard to forget about that poor dead woman.

The Submissive Scullery Maid
Shiralyn J. Lee

Lilly came in to clear the table and asked if Lidia wanted anything else. She told her that she was going to take a bath and asked if she could draw the water for her. Lilly immediately went to see to her employers demands. As she opened the door to leave, Lidia caught a glimpse of a young woman with beautiful red hair. She had just walked into the kitchen, so Lidia got up to see who she was. She had a strange feeling in her stomach, butterflies and sickness, yet it was pleasant and unnerving.

She whispered to Lilly as she returned to collect the rest of the china plates from the table. "Who's that girl, the one with the red hair?"

"Oh that's the new girl, her name's Sally, Sally McGuire." Lilly sniffed as she said her name in her cockney accent. "Now pardon me, Madam, I'll be clearing these plates up now."

"Thank you, Lilly, I will go and take my bath now." Lidia walked slowly up the stairs hoping to catch another glimpse at her new employee.

As she relaxed in her fragrant bath water, she closed her eyes and began to think about Sally. The new girl had excited her inner emotions and she needed to understand why. In just that one glance she had captured an image so pure, so innocent and yet she knew nothing about this girl apart from the fact that she had a similar look to Angelique.

She stroked the inside of her thigh and then ran her fingers over her belly and up to her breasts, caressing them as she thought about the girl and how she imagined being touched by her. The water swayed around her as she became amorous with her own body. She opened her legs slightly and placed her right hand over her private parts. She had one purpose in mind and using Sally as her visual, she began to play with her clit. Her hair hung over the end of the roll top bath tub and the sound of the water splashing got louder as she vigorously rubbed and teased herself. She wanted this girl, she needed this girl and she was going to have this girl. With her eyes closed, she envisioned

Sally's mouth in between her legs, tasting her juices as she gave herself to this beautiful creature. It took only moments before she came for her imaginary lover.

Over the next few weeks, Lidia's feelings had intensified towards Sally, she watched her every move as she would pass by in the corridor or clear their plates from the table after they'd eaten. Lidia had spoken to her husband about promoting Sally a few weeks back and he'd agreed.

With Lidia's secret liaisons with Cassandra, she was able to manage to act out her sinful desires. It was during one of their sessions that Cassandra suggested to Lidia that she should bring the girl along one day, just so that she could be humiliated in front of her. Lidia was reluctant at first but as she thought more about the idea, she soon had a change of heart and invited Sally to join them at the country house the following Sunday. It was to her delight that Sally agreed to accompany her and she secretly wished for the week to pass by quickly.

Cassandra met Lidia at her house and they entered the carriage knowing that they were going to pick Sally up just a little way down the lane. Lidia had asked her to make her pickup away from the house so that the other servants wouldn't be aware that something was going on. As they approached Sally in the lane, Lidia's heart began to beat faster, she could see her beautiful red hair shining in the sunlight. This was the most nervous she had felt in a long time and when she tried to remember when she last felt this way, she realised that it was the same feeling that she had held for Angelique. Her palms were clammy and her head dizzy with ideas that she would soon be in the arms of this beautiful girl. Little did she know that she was travelling towards the love of her life.

~The End~

About the Author

I began to write, because as a lesbian, there really isn't that much to watch on TV that suites my enjoyment. I have written several short erotic/BDSM stories and concentrate on ideas and situations that I find myself fantasising about.

As I finish one book, I find that I have already got ideas swimming around in my head for the next. And what I tend to do, is play the storyline out in my head for a few days as if I was watching a live play, with me being the producer and changing the scenes if I'm not happy with them.

Shiralyn J. Lee

The Submissive Scullery Maid
Shiralyn J. Lee

Published Books

Loving the Pink Kiss

The Dark Cully's Mistress

Pink Crush

Pink Seduction

The Submissive Scullery Maid

Vampire Changeling

Erotic Spirits

She's on the Ball

Ruby Tipped Globes

A Victorian Romance

The Dark Cully's Mistress

Paige Bleu Series, Case 321, Case 503, Case 16, Case 537

Sex, Ropes and Chains, Book 1, Book 2, Book 3, Book 4.

Printed in Great Britain
by Amazon

41810859R00088